SHERLOCK AND THE PERSIAN SLIPPER

The Early Casebook of Sherlock Holmes

Book Four

Linda Stratmann

Also in the Early Casebook of Sherlock Holmes
Sherlock Holmes and the Rosetta Stone Mystery
Sherlock Holmes and the Explorers' Club
Sherlock Holmes and the Ebony Idol
Sherlock Holmes and the Legend of the Great Auk
Sherlock Holmes and the Duelling Dukes
Sherlock Holmes and the Mycroft Incident

SHERLOCK HOLMES
AND THE
PERSIAN SLIPPER

Published by Sapere Books.

24 Trafalgar Road, Ilkley, LS29 8HH
United Kingdom

saperebooks.com

Copyright © Linda Stratmann, 2023

Linda Stratmann has asserted her right to be identified as the author of this work.
All rights reserved.

No part of this publication may be reproduced, stored in any retrieval system, or transmitted, in any form, or by any means, electronic, mechanical, photocopying, recording, or otherwise, without the prior written permission of the publishers.
This book is a work of fiction. Names, characters, businesses, organisations, places and events, other than those clearly in the public domain, are either the product of the author's imagination, or are used fictitiously.
Any resemblances to actual persons, living or dead, events or locales are purely coincidental.

ISBN: 978-1-80055-903-5

In memory of Thomas Simmons
1844–1885

From
Memoirs of a Medical Man
by A. Stamford FRCS

1924

CHAPTER ONE

It is not often that I am seen strolling with an attractive young lady on my arm, so on a bright but chill spring morning in the year 1877 I thought it might amuse my fellow students at Barts to give my visiting cousin Lily a tour of those parts of the college which she might find interesting. Lily and I have known each other since we were babies, and we are as close as brother and sister. She is a kind, affectionate girl, who likes to think well of others, and we have always been able to confide in one another. It was during this tour that we chanced to encounter Sherlock Holmes on his way to the chemistry laboratory, and I greeted him and made the introductions. He was clearly much preoccupied with a new experiment, and unprepared to stop and talk for more than a few moments. His manner was even more reserved than usual, and I saw in his eyes the fire of a great mind at work on higher things. After uttering the customary politenesses, he abruptly bid us good day and continued on his mission.

A little later, Lily commented, 'Your friend Mr Holmes does have such an intense stare, he quite frightened me!' As she did so, she pressed her hand over her heart as if to indicate an anxious fluttering in that organ.

'Oh, that's just his way, you know,' I said airily. 'He is a decent enough fellow.'

After a moment or two she asked, 'Is he a married or a single gentleman?'

Seeing the way things were going, I smiled and said, 'I believe he is very devotedly married to his work and likely to remain so.' My suspicions were correct as I saw her give a little pout of disappointment. Lily, although only a few months older than I, had already suffered two broken engagements, but undeterred, was clearly seeking another attachment.

It was soon apparent to me that the purpose of Lily's visit was more than merely cordial, and she had more pressing matters on her mind than the towering figure and aquiline features of Holmes. I decided to take her to a nearby tea shop, where I thought the comfort of a steaming beverage and a plate of scones might encourage her to unburden herself. After abstractedly consuming all the strawberry jam provided, she at last spoke.

'You remember Una, of course.'

'Miss Kenrick? Yes, I do. I hope she is well.'

Una Kenrick was a former schoolfellow of Lily's, and they had continued to meet and correspond over the years. She was a quiet, thoughtful, good-natured girl, and a gentle humourist in conversation. Her round, pleasing face was unfortunately marred by a large red birthmark, which crept up one side of her neck and extended over her jaw onto one cheek, where it rested like a gloved hand. Another girl might have been embarrassed by this and sought to cover it up in any way she could, but Una had a determined character and made nothing of it.

'Her life has not been an easy one. She has been alone in the world since her mother died, but she is intelligent and very capable. She used to keep house for an elderly gentleman, but the position did not suit her. When he passed away, she resolved not to continue in service, and found better employment with a linens company, managing their stocks and orders.'

'I am glad to hear she is settled,' I said. There was obviously more, and I waited.

'And then she had the most unexpected stroke of luck,' Lily continued. 'She received a letter from a solicitor who told her that a distant cousin, a man she had never even heard of, had passed away and since he had no direct heirs, she was the nearest relation. Of course, she was sorry to hear that he was no more, but all the same, there was good news to follow. This cousin had a property in Essex, in the village of Coldwell. And there was an investment in funds which provided a small income. Una was the sole inheritor.'

Despite this promising revelation, Lily continued to appear concerned.

'And she has received all the proper documents?' I asked. 'I mean, was it a genuine legacy, with no unusual conditions attached?'

'Oh, yes, everything was in order. She went to look at the house, and while it was tidily enough kept and there is a capable housekeeper, the furnishings are quite old, and the exterior has been badly neglected. She thought it too large for one person and made enquiries about either selling or letting it. And that —' Lily made a meaningful pause — 'that was how she was introduced to John Clark.'

I sensed that we had arrived at the nub of the problem.

'It all happened so fast,' exclaimed Lily. 'Una had never thought of being married; she did not think that was to be her life. Gentlemen — well, you know how gentlemen can be. If they liked her, and I know they did, they saw her as a servant, a housekeeper, a governess — never as a wife, and certainly not a mother. But when she met John Clark, she found him highly agreeable, and he thought the same of her. He is a man of property, recently retired from business, and was looking for a new home in the country. Before a few weeks had passed, they were engaged, and then married. The house, or at least those parts which are fitted out for their use, is now their home. They intend to renovate the whole in time, and it should be very handsome when done.'

'Did you attend the wedding?'

'No, it was a small affair as they are not yet able to entertain, but once they are, there will be a very grand wedding party.'

'Are you concerned that she may have made too hasty a decision?' I asked.

'I was, of course, but she wrote to me about her new life, and how happy she is, and how kind her new husband. And then, the letters stopped for a while. I waited to hear from her again. I hoped to receive an invitation to visit.' Lily took an unusually large gulp of tea that almost caused her to choke and dabbed her lips with the napkin. I refreshed the pot and poured more tea, and she returned to her cup eagerly. 'When I did receive another letter, it struck me as strange. Una said they were nicely settled, and making new acquaintances in the village, but intimated that her husband was more secretive about his past than she might have liked. She felt sure he had some sorrow which he did not wish to share with her. She did not like to press him on the subject and hoped he would enlighten her when he felt ready. In her next letter, she revealed that he was in the habit of going out on long walks in the countryside, alone. On one occasion she had found buttons missing from his clothes — not just lost, they were actually torn off, in a quite violent manner — which she had had to replace, and there was dirt clinging to his garments which had an odd smell she could not identify. She did mention it to him, but he brushed her enquiries aside, saying he had simply stumbled. As her letters continued, it was evident that she was becoming still more concerned about what he was doing, and the reasons for his continuing secrecy. She began to look amongst his effects for clues but found nothing. There was a drawer which he usually kept locked, but one day she found it open. What she saw inside shocked and frightened her. It was a pair of Persian slippers, one of which was stuffed with paper to keep it in shape, but the other had something in it.' Lily took a deep breath. 'Arthur — it was a gun. She dared not touch it.'

I decided not to mention that many men, including Holmes, own guns. In my friend's case, he was aware that his habit of delving into crimes placed him in danger from those who sought to put an end to his enquiries. Men who have served in the military often retain their service revolvers when they return home. Sportsmen might own several. Others simply like to collect them.

I did my best to soothe her anxiety. 'Perhaps it was simply an antique — a curio.'

'She didn't know. She did think of going to the police, but then she realised she had no proof of any kind of crime.'

'She may be worrying unnecessarily,' I said. 'I expect he will eventually confide in her.'

'Perhaps, but she also said that there were other matters concerning her husband which worried her, and she could not bring herself to commit them to writing.'

'You must have replied to her?'

'I did, of course, expressing my anxiety on her behalf, offering my help, and asking if I might pay a visit, but here is another thing.' I waited expectantly as she took a lace handkerchief from her glove and pressed it to her forehead and cheeks, as if to cool her emotions. I detected a powerful scent of rose petals. 'Una told me not to send letters to her at the house in future. I had to send them to the post office in the high street to be held until called for, and address them not to Una Clark, but Jane Dalton. That is her mother's maiden name. And she told me that I was not to visit her until she wrote to let me know that all her concerns were settled. And she also — she told me to burn all her letters.'

'Did you?' I asked.

Lily shook her head. 'I still have them.' Lily delved into her bag and drew out a bundle of letters tied with a piece of ribbon. 'I was going to show them to someone who could advise me. Would you take a look?' She bit her lip. 'Do you think it was wrong of me to keep them?'

'I think,' I said, cautiously, as I glanced through the pile of letters, 'that you may have done the right thing. And I have a suggestion to make. As you are so worried, might I have your permission to put the matter before my friend Sherlock Holmes, and show these to him?'

Lily gave a little gasp and looked suddenly more cheerful. 'Oh, do you think he would help me?'

'I can't promise it, but he has a remarkable mind, and can solve mysteries that baffle others. If he thinks there is something to be looked into then I will certainly undertake to visit Mrs Clark myself, and I hope that Holmes will agree to accompany me.'

CHAPTER TWO

Lily had some calls to make but agreed to visit me at my lodgings later that evening, and I went to see Holmes. As expected, he was inhabiting the chemistry laboratory. I found him engulfed in a powerfully acrid vapour, which gushed from a complicated arrangement of glass vessels and rubber tubing that occupied most of a bench. The threat of an imminent and catastrophic conclusion to his labours from liquid seething over the flame of a gas burner, was sufficient to ensure that he was not disturbed by other students, and he was alone.

I told him all I knew about Lily's concerns, and he listened politely. I often found it hard to discern how much attention Holmes gave to tales of woe. I sometimes received the impression that he had heard nothing at all or was listening only out of duty, while most of his concentration was directed elsewhere on subjects which he found much more interesting. Just as I was tempted to remonstrate with him for his inattention, it always turned out that not only had he heard and absorbed everything I had said, but he had developed fresh insights.

As I stopped speaking, Holmes stepped back from the bench and took out his pocket watch. 'I can give you a few hours this evening if your cousin wishes it,' he said.

It went without saying that we would meet in my rooms and not his, where there was a permanent fog of tobacco smoke. 'Thank you, Holmes, I will let Lily know. She is coming to me for supper at six o'clock. Do you think it might be a serious matter?'

'I cannot say at present,' he said lightly. 'There are some features which are suggestive, but I will not come to any conclusion until I have examined the letters. Kindly ask your cousin to bring them and, if she still has them, any letters she received from her friend in the months before her marriage, in particular those which describe her unexpected good fortune.'

He returned to his labours, and I perceived that our interview was at an end.

That evening Lily duly arrived at my rooms close upon the hour. Her complexion, on which she prided herself as being fashionably pale, was somewhat heightened either from the nipping breeze or the anticipation of seeing my friend again.

Holmes, who arrived bearing a volume of the Essex County directory, was calm and detached. He did no more than greet my cousin in a formal manner and request the letters. He did not, however, examine them at once, but placed them to one side, and asked Lily to tell him everything she knew about Mrs Clark while we made our simple supper.

Poor Lily tried to engage his closer interest without result. Throughout the conversation he barely glanced at her. It has often been said that Holmes did not like to associate with women, and to a degree this was true. Women were an unwanted distraction from the intellectual pursuits which dominated his existence. He was not impervious to female beauty, any more than he was to music or art, but music and art may be appreciated in a concert hall or gallery, as a welcome diversion from the toil of a busy life. A woman, had he joined his future with hers, would have been a constant intrusion which he would have found intolerable. An all-male company held no such dangers.

'We met at school,' said Lily. 'We were no more than seven years old. Poor Una has a port wine stain on her face, and while she does not allow it to affect her, I always feared it might influence her prospects. Some of the other children were cruel, and tried to make sport of her, and I came to her defence and told them they should be ashamed of themselves. That was how we became friends. Her father was a commercial clerk. He died when she was twelve years of age, and she was an only child. Her mother died about two years ago. But Una was determined to make her own way in life. She is intelligent, with clear, neat handwriting and an aptitude for figures. I was happy for her when she found a position with good wages.'

Holmes nodded and once the remains of our supper were cleared, he untied the ribbon binding the letters. He laid them out on the table, taking care to arrange them in date order, each resting by its envelope, then he took out his magnifying glass and examined them closely. 'You have no doubt in your mind that every single one of these letters was written by your friend?' he asked.

'None at all,' said Lily confidently. 'I know her writing very well, and it is more than that — there are little expressions she uses. And she has replied to the letters I sent her at the post office, so I know she received them.'

'This one,' said Holmes, tapping a paper with a long finger, 'is dated three months ago, and advises you of the unexpected inheritance.' He ran his glass carefully over the lettering. 'Her late cousin was called Roderick Brampton, and he was the headmaster of an elementary school in the village of Coldwell, Essex. A widower, with no living descendants.' He moved on. 'And in this next letter, we see that the initial anticipation at inheriting a cottage in that place has been somewhat dimmed by her visit, and the discovery that it is rather a run-down property. She has prudently taken advice from a solicitor in Ilford, a Mr Philpott. Mr Philpott introduced her to a Mr

Clark, a retired gentleman who had had a business dealing in fine furniture and whom he thought might consider purchasing or renting the cottage, as he believed it could be made very comfortable. Hmm.' The glass moved on. 'And here, scarcely three weeks later, we learn that Mr Clark is so enamoured of the young lady as to make his declaration. In another three weeks they are married. How extraordinary.' Holmes shook his head, though whether he was responding to the situation in particular or the general vagaries of human nature, it was not entirely clear. 'And now we come to the letters written after the marriage. It is the same handwriting, clear, firm, and without hesitation. A month passes without incident, only the usual commentaries on village life, and then the tenor changes. Yes, how very interesting. Of course, there are a dozen possible explanations for her observations and concerns, many of them quite unimportant.'

'What should I do?' asked Lily. 'I suppose I oughtn't to go there, as she has told me not to.'

'She has not told anyone else not to go,' I said. 'I am sure I could find some pretext to visit her.' I opened the directory. 'Is there anything of interest in that part of the county?'

'I really couldn't say,' said Lily. 'I think it is all farmland, and market gardeners. At least, there is nothing remarkable to speak of in Coldwell.'

My examination of the volume entirely confirmed that statement. 'I shall think of something,' I said. 'I have no further lectures to attend this week. I will go tomorrow morning. Holmes, would you be so good as to accompany me?'

'My laboratory work precludes me from doing so.' He looked at his watch. 'In fact, I must depart, as the next stage is due to commence soon, and I might be engaged most of the night watching over it. The warden of the college has already made known to me his opinion on broken glass and explosions, which is a considerable impediment to my endeavours.' He rose to leave. 'But do go, Stamford, by all means, and when you return kindly report to me all you have discovered.'

Lily looked disappointed, but she carefully folded the letters, returned them to their envelopes, bundled them in the ribbon with a neat bow, and handed them to me. 'Take them with you,' she said. 'Then Una will not be able to deny that anything is amiss, and you will be able to find out what has happened. At least you are someone she knows and will surely trust with the truth. Mr Holmes may well be correct; it might all be a silly misunderstanding. But if not, well, we will have done the right thing. I know she will be angry with me for not destroying the letters as she insisted, but if it comes to it, you may show them to her, and I will take the consequences. I am sure she will forgive me, as I have acted out of affection for her.'

As I made the preparations for my journey, I briefly entertained the thought of sending Mrs Clark a telegram to announce my visit on some weak pretext, but then I recalled that when Holmes wanted to discover what was being hidden, he liked to arrive unexpectedly, and take people by surprise. If Lily's friend really was in some difficulty, and was nervous of her husband, a telegram would have provided ample time for her to smooth things over and give a false appearance of all being well. I decided, therefore, not to forewarn her. To this day, I wonder, if I had sent that telegram, would things have turned out differently?

CHAPTER THREE

Mr and Mrs John Clark's address was Spring Cottage, High Street, Coldwell, Essex. The village lies only a few miles from Romford. Nowadays it is blandly urban in nature, but at the time of my visit, in the spring of 1877, Coldwell was a rural hamlet which merited less than a quarter of a page in the county directory. The meagre population, whose cottages straggled along the old coach road linking London and Colchester, mainly worked on the land, and there were the usual associated trades such as wheelwrights, and dealers in straw and poultry. A railway station had been opened in 1864, after which passenger coaches largely disappeared, and most of the road traffic consisted of farm wagons transporting produce. A few aged gentlemen, shunning the city and seeking country air, lived quietly in the better-appointed dwellings. The village boasted two hostelries, a chapel, a post office and grocery combined into a single business, an elementary school, and a resident constable.

I wasn't sure what I might find, or how long I would have to stay there. My enquiries might be concluded in a single visit over a pot of tea, or I might be asked to remain to be of some service. I decided to pack a small travelling bag, and I also carried the letters Lily had given me. I wanted to discuss them with Mrs Clark privately. I could not help but entertain the possibility that she had never sent them, and they were a prank by a clever forger, which was a mystery of quite another kind.

It was a period of highly unsettled weather, damp, cold and windy, its unpredictable nature much despaired of by farmers who were hoping to commence spring sowing. Outdoor amusements were always announced in the newspapers with the words 'weather permitting', not with any great anticipation that the weather would permit. Fortunately, my journey from Liverpool Street station was not a long one. I spent much of the way silently rehearsing how I might explain my unexpected arrival and wondering if I would be able to question Mrs Clark without her husband present. When I arrived, the sky was dense with cloud, and there was a threat of fresh rain in the atmosphere. I was the only passenger to alight at Coldwell. The ticket collector, his face ruddy and pinched with the chill and not taking any pleasure in his duty, gave me the oddest look, with a sharp glance at my bag, as if it might contain something suspicious. He said nothing, and it was easy for me to assume that strangers were a rarity in the area.

An unmade track bordered by hedgerows, which had been granted the title of Station Lane, led from the station to the high street, and I trudged along it, wondering what Holmes would make of it all if he was there, walking beside me.

The main street was composed of earth and grit, its surface rutted by the imprint of heavy wheels. On either side, narrow paths paved bumpily with stone sets permitted the passage of pedestrians. I passed a terrace of humble cottages, a row of small shops, the Plough Inn, a sprawling establishment rather faded from its old coaching days, and the post office and grocers where Mrs Clark collected her secret letters. There were few persons about, but those who were, instead of going about their business as I would have expected, were assembled in small groups, talking in low, confidential voices. As I passed by, they stopped talking and turned their heads to stare at me, then once I was out of earshot they began to talk again, more animatedly. Feeling increasingly uncomfortable with this reception, I walked on, past a low square building with a painted sign announcing that it was Coldwell elementary school. A recent addition to the sign revealed the headmaster to be a Mr Jas. Rowe. Beside it was a two-storey, double-fronted cottage. Although more substantial than those of labourers and artisans, it was far from inviting. The external brickwork, clothed with a heavy mass of invading creepers, was weathered and crumbling in places, and the window frames were cracked with age. A rusty gate bore the legend 'Spring Cottage.'

I pushed open the gate and walked along a stone flagged path which led to the front door. On either side were the remains of a garden, but what kind of a garden it had once been it was impossible to say, as it must have lain untended for a substantial number of years. I could not help but try and calculate the time and expenditure that would be required to convert Spring Cottage into the pleasant country home that Mr Clark had promised his new wife. Both struck me as a challenge. All was quiet, and although it was late morning the front curtains were closely drawn, and the windows shut. To my alarm, a group of villagers had detached themselves from their position across the street and followed me, going just as far as the gate, but not daring to enter, staring all the while. I had to wonder if all strangers attracted such keen interest, or if their pursuit was a sign of something else, something I had yet to discover. As I knocked at the door I was overcome by a creeping sense of dread, a fear that I ought never to have made this journey. Any hope that I was worrying unnecessarily vanished when the door was opened by a police constable. He did not appear pleased to see me.

'I have called to see Mrs Clark,' I said.

'What is your name and business, sir?'

'Arthur Stamford. Mrs Clark is a great friend of my cousin Lily Hargreaves, and she asked me to look in on her.'

His expression did not change. 'May I see inside your bag, sir?'

'Of course.' While he was rummaging through my linens, I said, 'Is Mrs Clark well?'

He closed the bag and handed it back to me. 'You'd better come inside. And make sure to use the doormat; the housekeeper is very particular about that, and I wouldn't want to get on her wrong side.'

I cleaned my boots as well as I could on a stiff bristled mat and stepped into a narrow hallway lined with drab faded wallpaper. A few small, ugly paintings did nothing to enliven the gloom. A woven, well-swept runner of some stout material was placed to catch any crumbs of the inevitable dirt that even the most careful visitor would have failed to dislodge. It was tidy enough, but underneath the scent of recent cleaning was an odour of decay, which in such an aged home could never be fully eradicated. The constable led me down the hall and, motioning me to remain where I was, knocked on a door. A man's voice answered, and my guide entered. I heard a brief conversation, then the constable emerged. 'The inspector will see you,' he said.

I found myself in a small parlour, mainly lit by the soft light of the cloudy sky seeping through a back window. I glanced outside, where I saw another neglected garden beyond which lay fields rolling into a misty distance. A coal fire glimmered in an iron grate. The simple furnishings included a table which was strewn with papers, while a flickering candle stub in a brass holder enabled the uniformed officer who sat there to pursue his work. He rose to his feet as I entered, and I saw before me a well set up man of about thirty-five, with close-cropped black hair and a neat moustache.

'Mr Stamford, take a seat,' he said. 'I am Inspector Mackie of Romford police.'

'Please tell me why you are here,' I begged him, as I sat down. 'I have only just arrived on the London train to see Mrs Clark, and I fear that something terrible has happened here. Is she —? I hardly like to say it.'

Mackie regarded me carefully, then resumed his seat. 'She is well,' he said.

That, at least, was a relief. 'May I see her?'

'Not at present. But I must ask you some questions regarding your visit here today.'

'Of course, I will tell you everything I know,' I said.

He opened a new page in his notebook and checked the sharpness of his pencil. 'I will first require your full name, your address, and your place of employment.'

I supplied all this information, which he copied down.

'How well do you know Mrs Clark?'

'I have only met her a few times, perhaps three or four. She was introduced to me by my cousin Lily. They have been close friends since schooldays. I escorted them to a concert once.'

'You would describe her as a friend?'

'An acquaintance.'

'You were never sweethearts?'

'Oh! No! Nothing of the sort, I assure you.'

'And what of Mr Clark? How well do you know him?'

'I have never met him. I only learned of the marriage yesterday, when Lily told me of it.'

'Have you been to Coldwell before?'

'No, this is my first visit.'

Inspector Mackie was writing notes of my replies, and then he leaned back in his chair and stared at his notebook, tapping the page thoughtfully with the end of his pencil. 'So, you are only slightly acquainted with Mrs Clark, and yesterday you learned that she was married to a man you had never met, and yet you have troubled yourself to make a journey to Coldwell, a place to which you have never previously been, bringing with you a few necessities which suggest that you anticipate staying here a short while. You have told me and Constable Higgs that you have come to see Mrs Clark at the behest of your cousin, who is a great friend of hers. Is that correct?'

'Er — yes.'

'Was she expecting you to call? She has not mentioned it.'

'She was not expecting it.'

Inspector Mackie gave me a stern look. 'Your cousin did not alert her friend to your arrival?'

'No. I don't believe she did.'

His look hardened, as did the grip on his pencil. 'Mr Stamford, I would be a fool not to see that there is more to this than you are telling me. Why did your cousin ask you to come here? Why did she not come herself?'

It was time to reveal the whole peculiar story. 'The thing is — and it may prove to be nothing at all — Mrs Clark wrote to my cousin saying that she was concerned about her husband's behaviour. He appeared to be very secretive. There may have been a simple explanation, but she was undoubtedly very worried. She told Lily not to send letters here, but to write to her care of the post office and begged her not to visit. Lily came to see me yesterday and told me what she knew, and how anxious she was, and I said I would come here and see that all was well. That is the purpose of my visit.'

'The sole purpose?'

'Yes. I am very fond of Lily, and I wanted to put her mind at rest.'

'Have you seen this letter?'

'Yes, there were several. I have them here. Lily was quite certain that Mrs Clark wrote them, but I still can't help wondering if it was someone playing a silly joke.'

Mackie did not perceive any humour in the situation. 'Let me see them, please.'

I took the letters from my pocket and handed them to him. They were not very long, and he read them, frowning a little as he did so. He had not asked me for Lily's full name and address, but I realised that the envelopes conveyed that information.

'Where did you spend last night?' he said, suddenly.

I thought this a little impertinent, but replied, 'In my rooms, of course.'

The impertinence continued. 'Alone or in company?'

'I was alone.'

'Can anyone vouch for you?'

'Lily visited me yesterday evening, but she left at about eight o'clock. I was alone after that. The next person who saw me was my landlady. My rooms are above her husband's bootmakers shop. This morning I saw her sweeping the front step and I greeted her as I went out.'

'What time was this?'

'About nine. Then I walked to Liverpool Street station to catch the train to Coldwell. The ticket collector will remember me; I was the only person to alight. Inspector, please tell me what has happened here. When I saw the constable, I feared something dreadful — has there been a burglary?' I had thus far seen nothing of value that a thief might covet, but there are desperate men who will steal trifles.

Mackie studied me briefly, as if trying to determine if my agitation was genuine. 'I would suggest to you, Mr Stamford, that you remain in Coldwell for at least another day, as I might wish to question you further. There is an inn on the high road, the Plough. I expect you passed it on your way here, and they have rooms at a reasonable cost. Will you undertake to do so?'

'Yes, yes, of course. And if there is any assistance I can give to Mr and Mrs Clark, they have only to ask.'

Mackie did not greet my offer of assistance with any enthusiasm. 'I will let Mrs Clark know that you have called. As to Mr Clark, I am sorry to say that last night at an unknown hour, he passed away.'

I think I gave a little cry of astonishment. And then I realised that the presence of the police meant that the death must be regarded as potentially suspicious, or at any rate worthy of close investigation.

'Was it an accident — or — don't tell me he — oh no, that would be too horrible.'

'That is to be determined. I am unable to say more at present.'

'Poor Mrs Clark. She must be distraught. And she has no close family.'

'She has been seen by a doctor who has given her a draught, and is now being looked after by the housekeeper, Mrs Pettigrew, who seems to be a very sensible person. Her solicitor has been informed.'

'Please let her know that I am staying in Coldwell and am at her service.'

'I will. I shall be continuing my work, as there are still enquiries to be made. I expect to remain in Coldwell certainly until the post-mortem is complete, perhaps longer, depending on the findings. The coroner has been informed and may well be in a position to open an inquest tomorrow. If I am required, I will be lodging at Rose Cottage, the home of Constable Higgs. It is part of the terrace near the station.'

I could not help wondering about the suspected cause of death. Had Clark taken poison? Shot himself while cleaning his gun? Had he been struck down by a burglar? I hoped for his wife's sake that some resolution could be arrived at without too much delay.

In the meantime, I had a vital duty to perform. I had to summon Sherlock Holmes.

CHAPTER FOUR

As soon as I was permitted to leave Spring Cottage, I hurried to the post office to send a telegram.

Milton's grocery shop and post office, being the only one of either ilk serving the village, had to be all things to all people, and therefore stocked a wide range of dry and preserved goods, cured meats, cleaning necessities, candles, lamp oil, patent medicines, sewing thread, buttons and stationery. As I made my way through an avenue composed of coarse sacks of rice and dried beans, I saw the counter I was seeking at the far end, and behind it a bespectacled grey-haired man attired like a clerk. I requested a telegram form, and as I completed it, Mr Milton, for I assumed this must be he, gave me a curious look of the kind to which I was already becoming accustomed. The look intensified when he saw the message:

To: Sherlock Holmes
Barts Medical College

John Clark dead. Please come if possible.
Stamford.
Plough Inn
Coldwell.

'Barts?' he said with a shake of the head. 'I'm not surprised. Bad business.'

'Yes, it is,' I said, hoping to hear more. He looked me up and down. At the age of twenty-two and looking rather younger, I was not well placed to give the impression of being a medical man of any degree of repute. Holmes, although scarcely a few months older than I, had height and gravitas and a confident bearing which enabled him to easily convince others that he was more than a mere student. 'Mr Holmes is a very able man and highly regarded,' I said. 'I am his assistant. His services are urgently needed.'

'I'm sure they are,' grunted the postmaster. 'Dr Wright has come from Romford to look at the body, and he is well thought of. But what with the police asking questions everywhere, and now a London man called in…' Another shake of the head. 'I don't know what went on. None of us do.'

'Did you know Mr Clark well?' I ventured. 'I have never met him.'

'No, they're new round here. Mrs Clark, she was Mr Brampton's cousin. He was the schoolmaster who died some weeks back. All he had went to her.' Mr Milton paused. 'Well, I won't say no more about that. It's a sore point with some. I expect you'll find out.' He had nothing further to say, and I paid for the telegram and went to the Plough Inn to await a reply.

The inn was probably the largest building in Coldwell. A wide carriage entrance led directly into a cobbled stable yard, and it was easy to imagine the days not so long ago when coaches laden with travellers and their luggage rattled in from London or the Essex coast. The yard would be bustling with ostlers hurrying to see to the horses, while passengers alighted to stretch their legs and take refreshment. The yard and stables remained busy, however, having been given over to the work of blacksmiths and farriers.

I entered the inn by the street door and found myself in a substantial public room with a long counter. Groups of men in working clothes were seated at tables enjoying a hearty midday meal of bread, boiled beef and beer. In one corner a slender gentleman in country tweeds with a smart walking cane by his side, sat alone with a small glass of beer and a beef sandwich. A folded newspaper lay on the table before him, and he was writing in a notebook. A man who I guessed was the landlord, a Mr Garbutt, judging by the name above the door, was a substantial and authoritative presence behind the counter. Aged about fifty or so, his high complexion and a banner of mottled flesh across his nose and cheeks demonstrated an enthusiasm for the local brew.

'Good day,' I said. 'I am looking for accommodation — do you have a room for hire?'

'I do.' He showed me a tariff. 'There is a daily rate and a weekly rate. With or without meals.'

As a student subsisting on an allowance from my parents, I was relieved to find that their charges were modest.

'I am not sure how long I will be staying. One day to begin with, and I will take my meals here.'

The arrangement was made, and after taking a key from a board, Garbutt opened a door behind the counter, thereby releasing a cloud of vapour and the savoury odour of boiling beef. 'Sarah! Room four!' he called out.

'Oh, and I am expecting a telegram,' I added when he returned. 'From a Mr Holmes of Barts Medical College.'

As I said these words, I saw a sharp movement out of the corner of my eye as the tweed-clad gentleman glanced up from his writing.

'Barts?' said Garbutt. 'Is he coming up to look into the death of Mr Clark?'

'Yes, at least I hope he will be free to do so. He is always very busy, as he is so much in demand,' I added, thinking it no harm to be generous with my praise. 'He has employed his expertise in many important cases. I am his assistant. I have already spoken to Inspector Mackie, but he is unable to tell me anything at present. I hope to learn more later.'

'All I know is that the man was found dead this morning and a doctor sent for, and next minute the police arrived. That's not the sort of thing we care for round here.'

'It's not,' said Sarah, emerging from the kitchen. She was neatly dressed in a plain frock and apron, and so similar in proportions and appearance to the landlord, although far younger and less ruddy of face, that I thought she must be his daughter. 'Constable Higgs usually has a quiet time of it.'

'Did you know the couple?'

'No, they never came in here,' said Garbutt. 'It was a big surprise to us all when the lady arrived, saying the house was hers.'

'Not to mention Mr Rowe,' said Sarah.

'The new schoolmaster?' I said, recalling the name on the noticeboard.

'That's him,' said Garbutt. He handed Sarah the key.

'I'll show you to your room,' she said.

We proceeded up some stairs and she unlocked a door. The lodgings were simple but clean. There was an extra charge for coals, and I said I might need a warm fire later in the day but for now, I would wash my hands and come downstairs for luncheon. A thought struck me. 'Why was Mr Rowe so surprised? Did he expect to inherit Spring Cottage? Was he related to Mr Brampton?'

'He was assistant master at the school before Mr Brampton died, and he was also Mr Brampton's son-in-law. Married the only daughter. He thought he would inherit through his wife, as there was a will leaving everything to her. Then Mr

Brampton was taken ill, very suddenly. He never spoke again and lingered on for six months before he passed. But before he died, Mrs Rowe died in childbed, and the babe too. Mr Brampton was too unwell to change his will, which he might have done if he had been able. When he died, Mr Rowe, not being a blood relative, got nothing.'

I knew that prudent persons in making a will often include a provision for disposal of their estate in the event of their main legatee predeceasing them, but it appeared that the schoolmaster had neglected to do so.

I arranged my things such as they were and went down to the bar, where I asked for food and drink to be brought. The tweedy gentleman was apparently engrossed in his newspaper, but after a moment or two, he laid it aside, rose, and came to my table. 'I hope you don't mind,' he said, 'but I would like to introduce myself. My name is Danbury. I am staying in the country for a short while, collecting interesting traditional tales. I had not expected to find a new drama in this very place.'

'Please take a seat,' I said. 'My name is Stamford.'

'And you work at Barts Medical College? Forgive me, but I could not help overhearing.'

'Oh, only in a very junior capacity.'

'This Mr Holmes, is he a senior man?'

I began to wonder if I had gone a little too far in my praise of Holmes and determined to be more strictly truthful. 'No, but he has experience beyond his years. He has acted as an assistant to Professor Russell in important cases.' Mr Danbury looked delighted at this revelation, and I could see eager enquiries preparing to spill from his lips. 'Of course, I am unable to reveal any details of his work,' I added quickly.

Mr Danbury closed his mouth and looked disappointed.

'Are you a newspaper correspondent?' I asked.

'No, nothing like that. I am a writer looking for stories to tell. I was passing through, but now I think I might stay a little longer and see what inspiration I can gather from the current circumstances. Oh, please don't be concerned, I will not intrude upon another's tragedy, but sometimes true events can form the foundation of a work of fiction. In fact, it is my intention when I have gathered enough material, to embark upon a novel.'

I thought then of the adventures I had already experienced with Holmes, the dangers, and the tragedies. I could not then share them with anyone else, but I was sure that any novelist would envy me my experiences and deem some of them too extraordinary, too marvellous, to ever be put in print.

Later that afternoon a messenger boy arrived with my telegram, and I took it to my room to open it. I had a feeling that had I opened it at once, Danbury would be looking over my shoulder. It was good news. Holmes was already on his way and would arrive in Coldwell by the next train.

CHAPTER FIVE

I waited for Holmes on the platform, feeling anxious right up to the moment the train arrived, and he descended, carrying a small travelling bag. My relief on seeing him may only be imagined.

'I am so grateful you have consented to leave your work,' I exclaimed. 'I know how much it absorbs you.'

He said nothing, but I could see from his grim expression and reluctance to discuss the matter, that the experiment he had been so determinedly engaged upon had been a failure and it had not been a great wrench for him to abandon it. I decided not to pursue the subject. He paused briefly, scenting the air and studying the cloudy sky, then hurried from the station.

As we walked up to the high street, I told him all that I had learned, which was little enough. 'I have not been permitted to see Mrs Clark yet, but she has been told that I am here. Inspector Mackie was rather suspicious about the reasons for my visit. I had to give him the letters to show him why I came here.'

Holmes paused in his stride. 'Ah,' he said. 'That is regrettable.' He walked on.

'I really had little choice,' I protested. 'But the letters may go to explain a great deal. If Clark has made away with himself, which seems one of the most likely circumstances, then they do suggest he had a sorrow which he kept hidden from his wife. Perhaps he'd received news that he'd lost all his fortune and was ruined.'

'We know nothing yet of the time or the manner of his death,' said Holmes. 'I will reserve any comment until I know more.'

We arrived at the Plough where Mr Garbutt, on learning that Mr Holmes of Barts had come up on the London train, responded with more alacrity and deference than my companion was expecting, and personally conducted him to a room rather superior to mine. Holmes was more than content to receive the attention and took care to say and do nothing to suggest he was not a man of some consequence. Mr Danbury, alerted by the bustle of activity, emerged from his room, and watched us like a naturalist peering from behind a bush to observe a rare species in the wild, hoping to see interesting behaviour. Finding that he had gained my attention, he waited in the hopes of an introduction, but was not afforded that pleasure. Holmes, having deposited his travelling bag, declined any refreshment and told the landlord that he would proceed at once to Spring Cottage, summoning me to accompany him with a brisk gesture.

'Who was that inquisitive fellow?' he asked.

'His name is Danbury, and he is lodging at the Plough. He says he is an author looking for ideas for a novel.'

'Avoid him,' said Holmes, with a curl of the lip.

'That will be hard to do.'

'If he is what he says he is, then we will be displayed to the public in horrid tales and indifferent prose. If he is not — all the more reason not to cultivate him unless it is to our advantage.'

By now a crowd of persons, on seeing that I had brought another stranger to Coldwell, had gathered outside the Plough and while they didn't dare interfere with our progress, they formed themselves into a body and trotted after us in pursuit.

As we approached the cottage Holmes cast his eyes over the rutted tracks of passing carts and the prints of booted feet and horseshoes. 'The wheels of farm vehicles obliterate all they pass over, which is unfortunate. I observe only that there has been considerable rain here in the last week, but, judging from the surface dryness and residues of water collected in the tracks, not in the last day.'

Eventually we stood at the head of the path leading to the cottage, with the gate firmly closed behind us. 'And now,' said Holmes, 'we may appreciate how the inclement and changeable weather has been our friend. See what signs may be observed, the age of which may be judged by the amount of mud and soil visitors have brought with them and how far it has dried. The path has been thoroughly swept by a well-wielded broom. I will need to discover precisely when this was last done. It leaves a clear canvas for footprints of varying sizes. I see yours, Stamford, which are a useful guide as I know when you arrived. There is a split in the leather of the sole of your right boot which should be repaired as soon as possible, or it will let in water.' He paused for a moment and looked about him. 'I will not use my glass to examine the path in detail until the crowds have departed, since any less obvious marks would be in danger of destruction if the curious decide to come and see what has attracted my attention.' He began advancing down the path, studying the surface as he proceeded, almost as if he was reading a book which revealed a story in a language that only he could interpret.

'Here we have two more sets of footprints, both of which are police issue boots. If I may venture a guess, I would say the well-worn boots are more likely those of the constable you mentioned, and the others belong to the inspector. See these? Another set of approaching marks, but smaller; the footwear is more elegant. This man arrived after the police. In all probability the doctor.

'If a servant ran to fetch assistance when Mr Clark was found dead, she would have emerged from the house with dry boots, so any slight marks she might have left on the path are no longer visible, but here we can see signs of her return: a small pair of stout boots which have been muddied by her errand.' He glanced up at the front of the cottage. 'You will have noticed the state of the ivy, of course.'

I decided to say nothing, since all I had noticed about the ivy was that there was a great deal of it, and this was not likely to prove a useful addition to Holmes's enquiries.

The door was opened by the constable, who, when Holmes uttered his name, adopted a more deferential manner, and admitted us at once, with the words, 'We have been expecting you, sir. Inspector Mackie is conducting some interviews at present, but he will be back to speak to you directly. Dr Wright is still engaged in the post-mortem on Mr Clark. Shall I show you up?'

'That would be very convenient,' said Holmes. He glanced at me, and I was sure he had deduced that I was responsible for his elevation in status. I had not advised the police of Holmes's arrival, but since the postmaster and the landlord of the Plough already knew, it was not hard to imagine that village gossip had carried the news faster than any telegraph. Holmes was experiencing something which had so far in his twenty-three years, been a rarity: fame and respect, and I feared that he was rapidly developing a taste for it. 'Mr Stamford is my assistant; his presence is essential to my work,' he added, generously.

'Of course, sir, come this way,' said the constable.

Holmes was not a student of medicine; his courses at Barts were anatomy and chemistry, but his private studies were enormous. He was especially interested in any subject relating to the understanding of the criminal mind and the detection of crime. I had often seen him in the college library absorbed in volumes of forensic pathology and studies of the abnormal brain, while sensational newspapers with their lurid accounts of horrible crimes were his regular fare. When John Watson described Holmes's examination of the bodies of murder victims, he was necessarily brief, as his great forte was short histories. He was more interested in the processes of the great mind as it solved mysteries than detailed medical notes. When I read his works many years later, I formed the idea that Watson, as a Doctor of Medicine, did not want to steal any of Holmes's thunder.

'You have been busier than is usual for you, I expect,' said Holmes, casually, as we proceeded upstairs.

'That I have,' admitted the constable.

'There must be many people who imagine that a village such as this will be an easy matter to police, but I am sure that even when there is not an incident of this nature, you are never wanting for all kinds of concerns to keep you occupied.'

'That is very true, sir. There are always reports of stealing, and I have to keep a lookout for young men prize fighting, and drunken persons thinking they can cross the railway line. I patrol the village every night, but there was nothing unusual to report last night. I passed Spring Cottage at about three o'clock and all was quiet then.'

'There has been nothing else out of the common way?' asked Holmes. 'I mean recently.'

'No, it's all petty squabbles, not that they are easy to manage. Mr Willans up at the poultry farm and his neighbour Mr Sharp are always quarrelling about something, and it's as much as I can do to stop them fighting each other, especially when they have been drinking. They've been on bad terms for years.'

'Let me know if something occurs to you that might be important for my enquiries,' said Holmes. 'In fact, I would like to hear of anything that strikes you as curious or unexpected.'

'I will do that, sir,' said Higgs.

We reached a poorly lit passageway, where the constable knocked on a door at the rear of the cottage, before announcing us. We entered a moderate sized bedroom, furnished with a single bed, a nightstand — on which stood a glowing oil lamp and the stump of an unlit candle in a brass holder — a wardrobe, a small writing desk furnished with ink, pens and a blotter, and a chair. The curtains had been drawn back to admit as much light as possible. The body lay on the bed, covered with a sheet.

'I am pleased to make your acquaintance,' said Dr Wright. He was a gentlemanly individual in a grey suit and refined yet serviceable footwear, well-groomed, with thinning hair and a trim beard. He was undoubtedly our senior by some ten or fifteen years and appeared rather surprised by our comparative youth.

'I have a letter of introduction from Professor Russell of Barts,' said Holmes, producing the document with a confident flourish. 'You will recall the recent unusual case of the poisoning of a boxer at which he gave evidence to the coroner. I assisted him in that case.'

'Oh, I do indeed,' said Wright. 'I read of it with great interest. Mr Holmes, I am indebted to you for coming here. Perhaps you would care to cast your eye over the remains?'

'Most certainly,' said Holmes.

Mr Wright drew back the sheet to uncover the upper part of the corpse, which was lying on its back, the arms loosely by the sides. We at last looked into the face of Mr John Clark.

CHAPTER SIX

The face of a corpse often gives little indication of the character and vigour that once animated the deceased. Nevertheless, a body has its own story to tell, if one knows what to look for, revealing not only the cause of death but the way that individual once lived. John Clark's features were relaxed and devoid of expression, the mouth a little open, eyes closed. I estimated that he was about fifty years of age, with thick, abundant hair of that unflattering hue when brown is fading to grey. There were prominent creases about the eyes and mouth, the lines left on a face that often smiled. Although beardless, he wore deep side whiskers and a luxuriant well-groomed moustache. He was clad in a nightshirt, the front of which was stained with a patch of blood surrounding a small, round hole. The material had been cut to give access to the doctor's instruments, the edges drawn together after the examination, but it was easy to see that there had been only a single wound to the chest.

'May I have more light?' asked Holmes, taking his magnifying glass from his pocket. I brought the oil lamp close, and he began his examination by studying the dead face, looking inside the mouth. 'I assume, Doctor, that you lit the lamp for your examination?' he asked.

'I did, yes. It was unlit and quite cold when I arrived.'

'And I observe that the candle had not burned down. Who discovered the body?'

'Mrs Pettigrew, the housekeeper,' said Dr Wright. 'She was sent to rouse him this morning, when he did not appear for breakfast at his usual time.'

'Was he found in this position, or has the body been moved?'

'Mrs Pettigrew said that she shook him a little by one shoulder before she saw what the matter was but did not move him. I found him lying on his back as you see him now. The covers were down at his waist, suggesting that he had been sitting up in bed and then fell back. And his right arm was extended towards the edge of the bed. I merely restored it to his side.'

Holmes had moved on to examine the hair of the corpse, parting the strands with the point of a pencil. This complete, he pulled back the cover fully and studied the folds in the sheets on which the body lay. 'There has been some movement,' he said, 'and I observe that while the left leg lies quite straight, the other is bent at the knee.'

'The cause of death is very apparent,' Wright continued. 'He was shot, a bullet in the chest which passed between the ribs and pierced his heart. There are no marks on either the upper sheet or the coverlet. The bullet did not pass through them, only the nightshirt.'

'Have you extracted the bullet?'

'Yes, I have it here. Most of the blood is in the chest cavity.' Wright showed us a saucer in which the bloodied projectile lay.

'A small-calibre weapon,' said Holmes.

'And the property of the deceased,' added Wright. 'It was found lying on the floor beside the bed, just below the position of the right hand. It was inside a Persian slipper, where I have been told it is usually kept. I have not yet completed my examination, but I am sure that the bullet was fired either from that gun or one very like it. It is not of a kind one commonly encounters. For reasons which you will see, I am as confident as I can be that this was the weapon.'

He brought a tray on which there lay a gentleman's slipper of soft brown leather, delicately embroidered in fine metallic thread. The toe curled up to a point in oriental style but was badly damaged by the passage of the projectile. Within it nestled a small pistol. The barrel and trigger were fully inside the slipper, and we were able to see only part of the grip, which was inlaid with mother of pearl and finished in silver with fine scrollwork engraving. 'The gun was discharged while inside the slipper,' he said. 'I have no doubt of that because there were some traces of leather and thread inside the wound which I was able to extract for comparison. As you see it is a very small, almost feminine piece. I will not withdraw it for examination, as the police will have their own experts better acquainted with firearms than I. It must be left as it is.'

I could see that Holmes was eager to examine the weapon, but he was forced to accept that he was not yet permitted to do so.

'Do you believe that Clark fired the gun himself?' I asked.

'It is just possible,' said Wright grudgingly, 'but only with great difficulty. I have probed the wound, which travels at a downward angle. The weapon was held most probably about one or two feet from his chest when discharged. He might have been able to fire the gun himself when he was sitting up in bed and holding it above his head at arm's length. But that is an extremely unusual position.'

'If he had been sitting up and looking straight ahead when shot, I think the gun would have remained on the bed, and not fallen beside it,' said Holmes. 'The position of the legs and arm suggests that his body was turned a little to the right.' Holmes was making a detailed study of Clark's hands. 'A man who means to shoot himself in the heart would press the barrel against his chest. But see here,' he added, 'there is a mark on the right sleeve from the passage of a bullet. Comparing the development of the hands and a small ink stain on the right forefinger, I deduce that he was right-handed. If he had fired the gun with his forefinger on the trigger, he could not have held it in such a way that it marked the sleeve of the right arm. He might have fired it with his thumb on the trigger, but why do so? His nails are short, but would he have been able to insert his thumb into the trigger guard of such a small piece? I would need to fully examine the gun to determine that. If he intended to destroy himself with such a light weapon, he would have been more likely to choose the temple, or the mouth. And why fire it from within the slipper?'

'Would that have muffled the noise?' I asked.

'It would,' said Holmes, 'but why did he wish to do so?'

'Mrs Clark and Mrs Pettigrew have both said they heard nothing,' said Wright. 'Mrs Clark sleeps in another room at the front of the house, and Mrs Pettigrew has a bedroom on the ground floor.'

'I will need to speak to them both,' said Holmes. 'Where is the other slipper? It must be one of a pair.'

'Yes, it is in the top drawer of the night table.' Wright opened the drawer, where we saw the undamaged matching slipper. 'Again, I have not touched it. I will leave that to the police. It has some rolled paper inside it, which I suspect may contain ammunition.' He closed the drawer. As he did so I saw Holmes compress his lips, and his fingertips quivered with frustration.

'I have taken samples of the stomach contents,' Wright continued. 'I don't believe there is anything suspicious there, but I will carry out the usual tests. I was told that he had dined, and taken a little wine, and was not in the habit of taking medicines or soporifics. Thus far I have observed no obvious signs of his having swallowed any harmful substances.'

'Were there no other signs of violence on the body?' asked Holmes.

'No, none. I have made a thorough examination.'

'Apart from the chipped tooth, the outer left incisor in the top jaw.'

Wright looked surprised. 'Oh, yes, but that looks like a very old injury.'

'It is. And I suppose you noted the shape of his moustache?'

'I — no. Does that mean anything?'

'It may mean something or nothing. I merely note it.' Holmes glanced about the room, and brought his glass into play once more, studying the floor. There was a small, plainly woven mat beside the bed, but in the rest of the room the flooring was varnished wooden boards, to which he gave special attention. He moved over to the window and examined the glass and frame very closely.

'What are you looking for?' asked Wright.

'Signs of an intruder,' said Holmes. 'The window is undamaged; there are no marks of fingers on the glass or footprints on the ledge. It is well secured from the inside. I can see that no-one entered this room by the window. Any other visitors have left nothing useful in the way of visible signs.'

'What do you think happened here?' I asked.

'I do not believe Clark shot himself, either on purpose or by accident,' said Holmes. 'The angle of the wound, his position in the bed, the distance between the weapon and his chest, all preclude it. He was not examining the gun. Had he been, there would have been a light in the room, but both the oil lamp and the candle were unlit when he died. He was shot by another person while sitting up in bed. Perhaps he awoke, sat up and turned his body to face the person who was standing by the bed, bending his right knee as he did so. That person held the gun in the slipper and fired it. Clark may have extended his arm to protect himself; he may even have tried to seize the gun. The rumpling of the sheets suggests a struggle. The bullet pierced his heart and he fell back. The person who fired the gun, and we cannot yet know if this was deliberate or accidental, dropped it on the floor and left.'

'Excepting only what my analysis may discover, I agree,' said Wright.

'Do we have any clues as to the identity of the assassin?' I asked, but it was apparent from the expressions of both Holmes and Dr Wright that there were none.

'Doctor, what is your opinion of the time of death?' asked Holmes.

'Judging by the cooling of the body and the temperature of the room, I would say approximately between midnight and four in the morning. But I could be wrong by an hour either way. I have been told that he retired to his room at about ten o'clock, although we cannot know when he went to bed. The body was discovered at about eight this morning, and it was then noticeably cool to the touch with some rigor apparent.'

There was a knock at the door, and the constable peered in.

'Mrs Clark has been told that Mr Stamford is here and would very much like to see him.'

'The grieving widow,' said Holmes as we left Dr Wright to complete his work. There was a mocking touch to his tone.

'Surely you don't imagine —?'

'It is what the world will think,' he said.

All I could think of, with a mounting sensation of discomfort, was those awful letters which I had, with the best of intentions, handed to the police.

CHAPTER SEVEN

Holmes and I joined Mrs Clark in the parlour. The fire had been made up and there was a tray of tea things on the table, but the widow appeared cold despite the thick woollen shawl wrapped around her shoulders. The housekeeper, a quietly efficient person, made deft work of pouring the tea, but seemed reluctant to depart. 'Thank you, Mrs Pettigrew,' said Mrs Clark, softly, 'you may leave us, now. I will send for you if we require anything.'

'I am so grateful to you for coming, Mr Stamford,' said Mrs Clark, once the housekeeper had left us. 'I had no idea that anyone in London had heard of my terrible loss. And Mr Holmes; Constable Higgs has told me of your generous offer of help, which is greatly appreciated.'

I hesitated, unsure how much I ought to reveal about the circumstances of my visit. The lady looked crushed and bewildered by her misfortune. I suspected that she was still affected by whatever draught the doctor had given her, which would have smoothed her more poignant emotions. 'I only learned of the tragedy on my arrival,' I said. 'I decided to pay you a visit at the behest of Lily. I saw her yesterday, and she told me she was concerned about your happiness here.'

'Oh,' said Mrs Clark, 'dear Lily, always so good and caring of others.' She reached a trembling hand towards her teacup but withdrew it, untouched. 'What can she have told you, I wonder?'

I glanced at Holmes, but his expression provided me with no inspiration. 'She said she had received some letters from you which suggested to her that you might have some worries on your mind.'

I waited to learn if my theory as to a forger or a cruel joker was correct, but Mrs Clark clearly knew to what letters I was referring. 'Oh, those silly things,' she sighed. 'I should never have written them. It was all down to a foolish fancy, and of no moment at all. In fact, I was about to write to Lily and reassure her that it was a misunderstanding and all my concerns had been resolved to my complete satisfaction. I hope she burned them as I suggested. It would be so embarrassing if anyone else was to see them.'

I saw Holmes lower his eyelids a little, his mouth pursed. If the situation had not been so terrible, I am sure he would have uttered a chuckle, or even a snort. 'Does this misunderstanding have any relevance to the events of last night?' he asked.

'No, none at all,' Mrs Clark replied, very insistently. 'Really, it is too trivial, too foolish to even mention. But I would so like to see dear Lily again. She is such a comfort.' The widow turned to gaze at me. There was no mistaking the anguished appeal in her expression. 'Please ask her to come if she can. She is my closest friend.'

'I will do so, of course,' I said.

'I would write, but if I so much as pick up a pen my hands shake so.'

There was a brief interlude during which Holmes and I sipped our tea, while our hostess sat silently with her thoughts. We put our cups down and continued.

'Mrs Clark,' said Holmes, gently, 'please tell me as much as you can about what has transpired here.' I saw her flinch. 'I am sorry to cause you pain, but I wish to understand the reasons for this tragedy. Perhaps you might begin by recounting how you spent yesterday.'

'Of course,' she said. We allowed her time to compose herself. 'It was a day like any other. John wrote some letters and posted them. He is — was — planning to make a journey to Wales next month to deal with some property matters there. And there are some trinkets that came with the house which he intended to have valued so they can be properly insured if necessary. We talked about the cottage and the plans to have it surveyed and the repairs attended to, and what improvements we wanted to make. He said I might have a free hand in selecting new furniture and drapery. There is a great deal to do.'

'Did you notice any difference in his manner?' asked Holmes. 'Did he have any concerns which he raised with you?'

'No, nothing like that. In fact, he was in a very cheerful mood. It was to be his birthday quite soon, and he told me that he had arranged for a nice little outing. I believe it was to be tomorrow. He had some business to attend to in Chelmsford, and he said that I should go there also, in company with Mrs Pettigrew to do some shopping, and once his business was done, we would all take tea at a fashionable hotel.'

'The housekeeper included?' queried Holmes. 'That is unusual.'

'He said she deserved a treat. He was very generous in that way.'

Holmes wrote busily in his notebook. 'If there are written notes of the planned works and other matters, I would like to see them. They may have no significance at all, but if that is the case it is as well to dismiss them from any consideration as soon as possible.'

'I am not sure I can help you, but there is a writing desk which I am sure has what you require.'

'I will not press you, of course,' said Holmes. 'My intention in examining his papers is to discover what property there is in Wales, who your husband's representative is there, his friends and acquaintances, and men of business who might be able to offer some information which will assist me. Has your solicitor been informed?'

'I didn't think to do it, but I must, of course.'

'According to Inspector Mackie, he has been told,' I said.

'Oh, I expect Mrs Pettigrew has done that.'

'Is there a will?' asked Holmes.

'I don't know.' Mrs Clark took a handkerchief from her sleeve and gently dabbed her eyes.

'If there is, it must be located. He may well have his own solicitor.'

Mrs Clark looked quite unable to deal with the crushing weight of the demands upon her. I proffered the untouched teacup, and she took it and managed to drink half the contents before returning it to me. We allowed her a moment, and after a while she rallied and looked a little stronger.

'Do you know what happened to my husband?' she asked. 'Mrs Pettigrew found him. She told me there was a wound on his chest, and a little gun which belonged to him had been fired. She thought that he would not have suffered. Poor John! I have not known him long, but he has been the most considerate of husbands. I can only think it has all been a horrible accident. He must have been examining the gun to see if it should be cleaned or valued and didn't know it was loaded.'

'Did you enter the room to see the body?' asked Holmes.

'Not at once. Mrs Pettigrew advised me not to. She said there was nothing I could do, and it would be best if the police came first. I went in later with Constable Higgs, but he said I should not stay, and he would arrange for the Romford police to come.'

'How long had your husband owned the gun?' asked Holmes.

'I don't know. It was quite old, and more of a decorative object than a weapon. Neither of us thought it was dangerous.'

'We will know more when Dr Wright has completed his examination and makes his report to the coroner,' I said.

'Has he told you anything? Does he believe it was an accident?'

I glanced at Holmes, unsure of what to say, but I think he knew that even the dreadful truth was better than the widow's worst imaginings. 'You must prepare yourself,' he said. 'Dr Wright is of the opinion, and I agree with him, that the gun was not discharged by your husband, but by another person. Whether accidentally or intentionally, it is impossible to say at present.'

Mrs Clark gasped in astonishment. 'But the only other persons in the house last night were Mrs Pettigrew and me, and we were both asleep in our beds.'

'A burglar, perhaps,' I said. 'Have there been any burglaries in Coldwell of late?'

'I don't think so. I have not heard of any. Constable Higgs would know, of course.'

'With your permission,' said Holmes, 'I would like to examine the cottage both inside and out to see if I can discover any possible means of entry. Mrs Pettigrew would be of considerable assistance in this. How long has she worked here?'

'She was formerly housekeeper to my cousin Mr Brampton. In fact, she cared for him in his last months. And please do whatever you feel to be necessary to establish the truth of what has happened. I will let Mrs Pettigrew know that she is to give you all the help she can. But I believed the house was secure from intruders. John was very particular about that.'

'Men can enter properties that are thought to be secure,' said Holmes. 'It is unusual not to leave signs of what they have done; it is only necessary to look for them.'

'When we took over the house, John said the locks at front and back were not good enough, and he had bolts put in.'

'Who did the work?'

'It was a local man; I don't recall his name. He was especially worried about the state of the back door, as the frame was warped with age, but I hope the bolt has corrected that.'

'Who else has been here since you inherited the cottage?'

Mrs Clark gave this question some thought. 'Mr Philpott, my solicitor. He came when I first visited to view the property. A delivery boy comes to the kitchen door, but he doesn't enter the house. And there is a woman who helps with the cleaning and laundry.'

'Did any builders or surveyors come to advise on the work required?'

'No, at least no-one who entered the property. Oh, and I have just remembered the dreadful Mr Cutter. He is a dealer in second-hand goods. He came here before I was married and looked around and offered me a sum for the entire house contents. Thirty pounds, I think he said. I did not think him very trustworthy. I may not know much about chinaware and plate, but I know when someone is trying to cheat me. I declined Mr Cutter's offer, but he left a card. That was when I started to make an inventory. Many of the items, if cleaned, will look very attractive on display. Mr Philpott said I wasn't to sell anything until the contents had been properly valued and when I met John, he advised the same. Too many businessmen think they can take advantage of a single woman. But then once I was married, the furniture and effects became John's, and I think he would have sent Mr Cutter away if he had returned. The only other visitor was Mr Rowe, and he was not very pleasant.'

'The schoolmaster?' I said. 'I was told his story. What did he want?'

'He claimed that there was something my cousin had intended him to have, and he wanted it. Oh, he started out friendly enough, smiling, persuasive. He said it was of little monetary worth but had sentimental value. Naturally I only had his word for that and was not going to take it without advice.'

'Did he mention a specific item?' asked Holmes.

'Yes, there was a watch that had belonged to Mr Brampton's grandfather. I said I could not hand it to him without proof that he was entitled to it, and then his manner changed. He said he was thinking of contesting my cousin's claim, and if he succeeded, I would have nothing at all, but he would not do so if I gave him what he considered to be his by right. I told him I would consult my solicitor and asked him to leave my house. He became angry, and threatened to go to law, but I stood my ground, and he went away. Mrs Pettigrew has orders not to admit him again.'

'Who has the keys to the house?'

'John and myself and Mrs Pettigrew. No-one else, as far as I know.'

'What of Mr Rowe's late wife? I assume she must have lived here prior to her marriage. Did she have a key? If so, Mr Rowe might still have it.'

'Oh, I see. I don't know.'

At that moment Mrs Pettigrew entered to see if there was anything else needed. She saw that her mistress was almost too weary to go on and took charge of her at once. 'There now, that's enough, you need your rest.'

Mrs Clark grasped the housekeeper's supporting arm. 'Mr Stamford and Mr Holmes want to speak to you. Please assist them in any way you can.'

Holmes rose to his feet. 'If I might trouble you, Mrs Pettigrew, when Mrs Clark is settled, I would like a tour of the house.'

'Very good, sir,' said the housekeeper, and removed both her mistress and her half full teacup from the parlour.

The pot was still warm, so I poured more tea. 'I haven't seen any obvious signs of an intruder,' I said. 'Broken windows; forced locks. Surely the police would have found something as plain as that by now?'

'They would, yes,' said Holmes. 'Either we have an intruder who was remarkably skilled at concealing his work, or Mr Clark was shot by someone who was already in the house, either as a resident or a visitor.'

CHAPTER EIGHT

'You don't imagine that John Clark was shot either by Mrs Clark or Mrs Pettigrew!' I exclaimed.

'I cannot rule it out,' said Holmes, calmly.

'I will not believe it!'

'Or he was shot by another individual who entered the house with or without the knowledge of those living here. And from what I have seen so far, this is not a house where doors and windows are carelessly left open for anyone to enter.'

'Do you mean the killer might have been someone either Mr Clark or Mrs Clark or Mrs Pettigrew knowingly admitted?'

'Not Mr Clark, I think, unless he was in the habit of receiving visitors while clad in his nightshirt and in bed.'

'Nothing would surprise me,' I said, 'but yes, it is unlikely. It must have been a burglar. Both the ladies have said they were in bed asleep when Clark was shot.'

Holmes gave me a veiled look.

'Oh, I see what you mean,' I said. 'If they were involved, however innocently, they might not choose to say so. But who might they have allowed into the house at night? Why would they do so?'

'Especially as Clark made sure to have bolts put on the doors as soon as he took up residence,' said Holmes. 'I wonder — did he have something specific to protect? Something of value? A secret? What was he afraid of? Or was he simply an unusually nervous man? It is not as if Coldwell is a hotbed of serious crime. The very seclusion might have been what recommended it to him.'

'If one of the ladies had admitted someone, however innocent the purpose, she would have been awake, and heard the shot, and alerted the constable,' I said.

'Unless the visitor came much earlier, and stayed late, and neither lady has seen fit to mention it. The other possibility I must consider is that an intruder somehow negotiated both locks and bolts, committed the crime and left the house, leaving no signs that he was ever here. At least, no signs that the police have yet discovered.'

'That is what you mean to look for.'

'It is a curious case. I must miss nothing.'

Mrs Pettigrew returned and awaited our instructions. I saw before me a sombrely dressed female aged between fifty and sixty. She was as composed as it was possible to be under the circumstances. I wondered if she had witnessed both the collapse and death of her former employer, Mr Brampton. I knew she had been his nurse between those two events. I judged her to be capable of facing such contingencies without making a fuss. It is a mistake made by so many — and I am sure that before I met Holmes, I was as guilty of it as anyone — to pay no heed to servants. But servants see and hear things that others do not. The best servants know everything and say nothing. What information or insights might Mrs Pettigrew have that she would be prepared to reveal to us, or choose to conceal, despite the instructions of Mrs Clark?

'How might I assist you?' she asked.

'First, I wish to know when the path was last swept,' said Holmes.

If she was surprised by this question, she did not show it. 'Yesterday afternoon,' she said. 'A woman comes once a week to help with the laundry and rough work, and that is one of her duties. A Mrs Webster. She does all the paths and steps, back and front.'

'And I believe it has not rained here since then?'

'It has not.'

'Does Mrs Webster have a key?'

'No, when she is to do the indoor work, she comes to the back door, and I let her in.'

'I understand it was you who found the body of Mr Clark?'

'Yes. He usually rose at about seven and breakfasted at eight o'clock, and when he did not appear Mrs Clark asked me to go and see where he was. She thought he might have gone out to take the air. When I went into his room he was still in bed, and when I called him, he did not respond. I feared that he might have been taken ill. I drew the curtains and went to try and wake him, and then, of course, I saw that he was dead and there was blood on the front of his nightshirt. I told Mrs Clark that I had to fetch someone, and then I went to see Constable Higgs, who is the nearest help.'

'The lamp and candle were unlit?'

'Yes. It was not necessary for me to light them once the curtains were drawn.'

'Did you notice anything in the room that had been moved or disturbed? Any marks on the floor?'

'The first thing I noticed was that the top drawer of the nightstand had been pulled out and not put back. He always kept the drawer closed. As to marks on the floor, I am not sure I looked for any.'

'Did you see the gun?'

'Yes, it was lying on the floor beside the bed, still inside the slipper where he kept it.'

'Did you touch it or move it?'

'No. I thought the police would want to see it where it lay.'

'What was your first impression of what had happened?'

'I thought he must have shot himself. I still do. Gentlemen can sometimes be careless with guns, which they see as playthings and do not think them to be dangerous. Or maybe — and I am sorry to say this and would not dare suggest it to Mrs Clark — maybe he did it on purpose. Like George Makeham the bonnet maker, four years ago. He was found dead in his bed, shot though the heart. And the rumour in the neighbourhood was that he had been murdered for his money. Then when it was looked into, it was found that his lady friend had deserted him, and he had more bills than he could pay, and it had affected him very strongly. Perhaps Mr Clark had secrets we don't know of which drove him to it.'

'Where did he usually keep the gun?'

'In the drawer of the nightstand. There is a pair of Persian slippers, and the gun is kept in one and the bullets in the other. I am not sure he knew it was actually loaded.'

'He did not say how he came by the gun and the slippers?'

'No, I think there was some mention of gifts from a friend who was well travelled. That is all I know.'

'Mrs Clark has told us that as far as she is aware, the only persons in the cottage last night apart from herself were you and Mr Clark.'

'That is the case.'

'You did not admit any visitors?'

'I did not.'

'Are there any persons, such as friends or relatives of yours, who you might admit as your personal visitors, perhaps to the back kitchen, without Mr and Mrs Clark being aware of it?'

Mrs Pettigrew's posture stiffened. 'I am friends with Mrs Acton, a very respectable person, who is housekeeper at the Old Manor House. My only relatives are a sister, Mrs Barnes who lives in Ilford, and a nephew, her son Clem, who now lives in London. I would never admit anyone to the house without the knowledge of my employers. It is not my place to receive personal visitors.'

Holmes rose to his feet. 'Thank you. And now I would like you to show me the house.'

'What is it you wish to see?' she asked.

'Everything,' he replied.

'Not all of the rooms are in use,' she replied. 'But you are welcome to see them all.'

'Tell me what you know about Mr Clark,' said Holmes, as we proceeded into the hallway.

'He was a gentleman of regular habits,' she said. 'He wanted everything done just so, which made my work easier as I could anticipate his requirements. In this he was quite unlike Mr Brampton, who, surprisingly for a schoolmaster, was not so well regulated. But then Mr Brampton had his foibles, and he could be excused them as he was well-liked.'

'Foibles?' queried Holmes.

'The contents of his medicine cabinet spoke for themselves. I will say no more.'

I said nothing, but during my studies at Barts I had often attended the post-mortem examination of persons whose medicine cabinets showed an unusual enthusiasm for such things as brandy and laudanum.

'How old was he when he died?'

'Fifty-eight. He was teaching a class when he suddenly fell to the floor and had to be carried home. He never spoke a word from that day until the day he died.'

Mrs Pettigrew selected a key from the bunch at her waist and unlocked the door of one of the front rooms. It was sparsely furnished with a dingy sideboard and armchairs, and a few unremarkable china ornaments and brass candlesticks. 'I do not think this has been used for some years,' she said. 'Miss Brampton — Mrs Rowe, as she later was — used to sit here sometimes, when the light was good, and I made up a little fire for her. She liked to read and draw. But then Mr Brampton put a stop to it, as he said he could not approve the price of the extra coals.'

'Did Mr Clark reveal what plans he had to renovate this house?' asked Holmes, as he walked about the room, examining its contents and paying particular attention to the window.

'No, only that it was his intention to do so.'

'Did he invite surveyors, architects, builders, to examine it, and put a price on the work?'

'Not that I am aware of. He might have consulted with them, as he went up to Ilford on business from time to time. Although I understood that the work could not proceed until he had sold one of his properties to finance it. But I did say to him, because I had also warned Mr Brampton, that the first thing that needed seeing to was the drains. Mr Brampton said he would look into it, but that was just before he was taken ill. And the winter only made them worse.'

'But it was Mr Clark who asked for bolts to be placed on the doors?'

'Yes, he was not satisfied with the security provided by the keys alone. The back door lock was hindered in its working by a movement of the door frame. He had bolts added, both front and back.'

'Who carried out the work?'

'Sam Empson, the blacksmith. He has a workshop in the coach yard of the Plough.'

'I assume that the house is both locked and bolted at night?'

'It is. I do it myself, every night at ten o'clock, without fail.'

'And when is it unlocked?'

'At six o'clock, when I see to the fires and begin to prepare breakfast.'

'And this morning, did you find all the locks and bolts secure and untampered with?'

'I did. Both front and back doors were locked and bolted exactly as I left them last night.'

'And can you confirm that at ten o'clock last night, the only persons in the house were Mr and Mrs Clark and yourself?'

'Yes.'

'If, for whatever reason, however innocent, another person was admitted, and you are reluctant to say so, I would understand, but if it was later discovered that this information had been concealed, things would go very badly for you,' said Holmes.

Mrs Pettigrew showed no signs that this advice caused her any difficulty. 'I admitted no-one,' she said, 'and will gladly swear it upon the Holy Bible.'

'That will not be necessary,' said Holmes. 'Did the delivery boy come as usual this morning?'

'Yes.'

'What did he bring?'

'Vegetables and eggs. He puts them into a basket on the back doorstep.'

'And what time did he make the delivery?'

'I couldn't say. He usually comes shortly before six o'clock.'

'How many keys are there to the house?'

'There are three to the front door. I have one.' She patted the chain at her waist. 'Mr Brampton had one and that was passed to the possession of Mrs Clark when she inherited the house. The third one was for the use of Miss Brampton when she lived here. Her father held that one, too. She did not take it away when she married. I think it is the one which is now on Mr Clark's key chain. There are only two keys to the back door. I have one and Mr Brampton had the other. There was no reason for Miss Brampton to have one. I think Mrs Clark has the second one, but she may have passed it to Mr Clark.'

'What age was Miss Brampton when she married?'

'She was twenty-six.'

'Are you saying that she was not allowed to hold her own front door key before then?'

Mrs Pettigrew seemed reluctant to criticise her former employer. 'It is unusual, I know. Her father was very protective. She would sometimes go out to take the air or visit the shops with a friend, a widow lady, Mrs Harmon, who is Mr Rowe's sister, but her main occupation was helping her father with his papers.'

'This window is very secure. I imagine it has not been opened for some time,' observed Holmes.

'Yes, it is opened occasionally to air the room, or it would get very musty, but it is closed most of the time. Mr Clark inspected all the windows when he came here, but he appeared to be satisfied that no repairs or additional locks were needed.'

'Forgive me, but I must ask about the sleeping arrangements. Mr and Mrs Clark do not share a bedroom, although it is a small house. Is there a reason for this?'

'Mr Clark said that he was a light sleeper and did not wish to be disturbed by the noise of the farm carts going back and forth along the high road at all hours. Mrs Clark was happy to allow him to take the back bedroom for this reason, especially as she was able to sleep in the larger front bedroom, which she preferred. She is a sound sleeper and did not think she would be disturbed.'

'Which bedroom did Mr Brampton occupy when he lived here?'

'The front bedroom, and Miss Brampton was at the back. The little writing desk was once hers, where she sat and worked on her father's papers.'

I thought of poor dead Miss Brampton, who was not permitted her own door key, whose father was reluctant to buy enough coals to keep her warm, and who once married was not afforded the joy of motherhood before passing away. I wondered about the life she had led in Spring Cottage, and if she had ever been happy.

CHAPTER NINE

We had just emerged into the hallway, which Mrs Pettigrew said led to a back parlour and kitchen, when Constable Higgs opened the door to admit Inspector Mackie. 'Mr Holmes of Barts is here,' said the constable.

'Indeed,' said Mackie, not in the friendliest manner. I saw him study Holmes, as if trying to judge his age and experience. I rather hoped he would not demand to know what qualifications my friend possessed, as he had none. Holmes did not even have a degree, as he had left college before his final year, to pursue those studies he thought would be more useful. It would be some time before the world recognised that Holmes's brilliance went far beyond the mere passing of examinations.

'Mrs Clark has kindly agreed to allow me to inspect the house,' said Holmes.

'Oh, and how much of it have you inspected so far?'

'Only the one room,' said Mrs Pettigrew, locking the one we had left.

'Then I am back just in time,' said Mackie.

'I have a letter of introduction from Professor Russell of Barts,' said Holmes, producing the document. 'Dr Wright has already approved it.'

The inspector did not trouble himself to read the letter. 'Then you may assist Dr Wright in a medical capacity and Mr Stamford may offer assistance to Mrs Clark as a family friend, but that is as far as I can allow. Neither of you are police officers; neither of you are authorised or instructed to do police work. I have already inspected the house for myself, and

I intend to order a close scrutiny by professional advisors approved by the police. I hope they will not discover that anything has been tampered with.'

'I can assure you, Inspector,' said Mrs Pettigrew, firmly, 'that the gentlemen have done no more than inspect one room and have not "tampered", as you put it, with anything.'

'Is Mrs Clark about?' asked Mackie.

'She is resting,' said the housekeeper. Her tone suggested that this state of affairs would continue until she said otherwise.

'Well, I won't disturb her,' said Mackie, 'and I would be obliged if you two gents could take your leave now.'

We had no alternative but to comply. As we stepped out of the front door, we saw that the assembled cluster of villagers, possibly at the insistence of Inspector Mackie, had departed about their business. Holmes turned and looked up at the thick carpet of ivy that all but occluded the brickwork of the wall that faced the street. Then he seized a snaking branch and shook it. He pulled off a leaf, examined it, smelled it, then crushed it in his fingers. Walking across the front of the house he at last found the thick root, the origin of the whole, and knelt to look at it. After a few moments, he stood and pulled at the wiry branches, causing some of them to come away from the wall. I waited for him to say something, but he only looked thoughtful and returned along the path to the front gate, looking at the neglected garden.

'I hope the inspector will not prevent me from examining the paths,' he said. 'I had better do so now in case of rain, which I do not think will hold off for too much longer.' Holmes employed his glass and crouched to proceed gradually down the path. It was a posture which uninformed observers often regarded with amused derision, before claiming his discoveries for themselves.

'Do you detect any signs of another visitor?' I asked.

'I do not, but if he made any light marks they might not have been noticed and have since been occluded by the muddy tracks of later arrivals.' Holmes rose to his feet and stared about him. 'There are no tracks through the garden; the soil is not disturbed. However — I think I see something.' He bent down again, and by the side of the path he examined and then picked up what appeared to be a short length of some coarse thread.

'What have you found?'

'Hessian, I believe, a fragment from the weave of some sacking. Dry, and lying on the surface where it might have been blown by the breeze. Recent, therefore. Possibly even from last night.'

'A burglar, bringing a sack to take away stolen goods?' I suggested, since it had occurred to me that the gun and the watch might have some value.

'Perhaps,' said Holmes, thoughtfully. He continued along the path and, drawing near to the cottage door, examined the front steps. Turning to his right, he carefully studied the pathway that wound around the side of the building, which was just wide enough to allow one man to pass to the rear of the cottage. 'Nothing I might follow,' he murmured, 'the faintest traces that can barely be seen and would not amount to convincing evidence of anything. Yet I am sure now that there was someone here.'

At the rear of the cottage, he paused and stared up at the wall, paying particular attention to the area below the window of John Clark's bedroom. The ivy must have been abundant there once, but unlike that at the front, only stumps of the main trunks remained. The tendrils springing up the wall were new growth, their thin vine-like stems reaching only to the top of the ground floor windows.

Mrs Pettigrew's concern about the drains was immediately understandable. An unpleasant odour pervaded the area, not the sharp freshness of a garden returning its old vegetation to the soil, but of something offensive dissolving into slime, the sickening, acrid taint of untreated sewage.

The entrance to the kitchen door, which was approached by two shallow stone steps, was kept dry by a small covering porch. On the top step was a wicker basket with a lid. Holmes looked inside but it was empty. Even without a close inspection of the door, it was possible to see the distortion of the wooden frame which had caused the mortar to crack. A thief who was simply looking for opportunities might have believed it could be opened easily, but if he had tried to do so, the combination of lock and bolt would surely have defeated him.

The rear garden, which I had previously observed from the parlour window, was an abandoned rectangle of earth, bisected by a simple path of irregularly shaped flat stones. Parts of it were sunken into muddy pools, which I hoped Holmes did not mean to explore. At the far end was a wooden shed, one wall of which had collapsed, the roof adopting a lean which threatened to slither to the ground and form a pile of rotting planks.

One section alone of this abandoned wilderness was well tended and productive. Not far from the kitchen door was a small plot surrounded by a miniature fence made of woven branches and planted with herbs of several kinds. I am not especially knowledgeable about culinary plants, but I recognised bushes of rosemary and thyme. A series of markers had been placed in the soil, the sort one sees in botanical gardens to inform visitors, with names impressed on a thin metal plate.

Holmes stared at the garden, then bent down, and brought up something with a little cry of triumph. 'Yes, a small thread of hessian blown by the breeze has caught against the fence.' He studied it through his glass. 'If I am not mistaken, it is of the same type as the first one, but of course sacking is a common enough material, so it may be hard to draw any conclusion.'

Holmes was about to continue his searches with a closer examination of the door, when we heard a little chuckle behind us, and turned to see Inspector Mackie leaning against the wall, smiling. 'I know a persistent man when I see one,' he said. 'Now, I suggest you both be on your way. And if you do not leave, I am afraid I will have to insist.' He spoke politely, but there was a world of meaning in the word 'insist' which I hoped never to explore. Even though he was impeding Holmes in his work, he struck me as a pleasant enough fellow who was only doing his duty.

'Very well,' said Holmes, 'but I will observe that the ivy at the back of the house was cleared several years ago while that at the front has only recently been cut, most probably with the intention of allowing it to die back for easier removal.'

'So I see. Your point being, which has already occurred to me, that if there was an intruder involved, he could not have climbed up either back or front to enter through a bedroom window,' said Mackie. 'In fact, I think we can entirely rule out anyone having entered the house last night through a window.'

Holmes said nothing in response to this. If he had his own conclusions, he was not about to share them. 'I believe that there was another visitor during the last day who came to the back of the house. I have found some threads of hessian, one by the front path and one just here.'

'You have sharp eyes, Mr Holmes. If you decide to apply to join the police force, I will certainly recommend you. That visitor was almost certainly the delivery boy who brings eggs and vegetables from a nearby farm.'

'Does he pull a little handcart?'

'Yes, have you seen him?'

'No, but I have seen tracks made by a handcart just outside the gate. The farm carts have rolled over them, but there were enough remaining. Mrs Pettigrew did not see him, however; he left the delivery on the back doorstep before six o'clock.'

'We mean to speak to him, as he may have seen or heard something of interest. Are you done now, sirs?'

Holmes had not done, but he must have judged that it would not assist his progress if he antagonised the inspector. 'I am making a scientific study of footprints and hope to publish a monograph. Have you been able to find any marks made by the delivery boy as he left?'

'I expect his movements will become clearer when I speak to him. The one thing I do not wish to do is explain to the Chief Inspector why *your* footprints are all over areas that do not concern you. Now please leave.'

'Very well. But let me know when we may return to see Mrs Clark. She requires assistance with the necessary arrangements. I am to be found at the Plough Inn.'

As we walked away, Mackie took care to watch us go. Holmes paused outside the gate for a closer examination of the tracks of the handcart, which he determined had stood outside the house for a short while before moving away up the road. 'It seems likely that the delivery boy was here after Mr Clark was killed. Even so, there is a good chance he witnessed something.'

Holmes remained thoughtful and silent on the subject of the hessian. He liked to exercise his bloodhound-like abilities, and often they led him to vital pieces of information. But on this occasion, I suspected, as did the inspector, that he had simply observed something commonplace, which had nothing to do with the death of John Clark.

'I had better send a telegram to Lily,' I said. 'I am sure Mrs Clark will find her a great comfort.'

'Once that is done, let us find Mr Empson, and talk about the bolts,' said Holmes. 'I can see where the inspector's deliberations are aimed, and I am not convinced he is looking in the right direction.'

CHAPTER TEN

At the post office, I composed a carefully worded telegram asking my cousin to come to Coldwell. I made sure to request that she let me know what train she was taking, so I could meet her at the station. I thought it inadvisable in the circumstances for her to go directly to Spring Cottage and determined that I should break the dreadful news to her before she went to see her friend.

'Mr Holmes, is it?' asked postmaster Milton, staring at my companion, who was examining a sack of beans with his glass. 'Are you the gentleman from Barts?'

'That is I,' said Holmes. 'I have been called in to assist Dr Wright.'

'You've seen the body, then?' asked Milton. 'How did he die?'

'We are still investigating, and while we do so, we are advised to say nothing until the inquest receives our report,' said Holmes. 'All I can say is that Mr Clark is undoubtedly deceased.'

Milton gave a dissatisfied grunt.

'I expect that anyone who saw or heard anything of note last night will be called as a witness by the coroner,' added Holmes.

'No-one here has, or I would have been told about it,' said Milton, with a sour grimace. 'All of us were asleep in our beds. That inspector has been round every house asking questions, but he's none the wiser.'

'I expect Mr Clark was a good customer of yours,' said Holmes. 'A man of property, of business. I am told that he used to write many letters.'

'He was never in here,' said Milton. 'Mrs Clark came in sometimes to buy stationery and collect letters from London for an aunt of hers. Dalton, the name was. Though why her aunt couldn't send them to Spring Cottage, I never could understand.'

'You say that Mr Clark did not send letters or telegrams?' asked Holmes.

'Not here, no. I did wonder if he might have had business elsewhere. Some of the gentlemen in the big houses, they go up to Romford or Ilford by train to see their bankers and legal men. I don't know what Clark's business was, but I heard he was a man of means. Mrs Clark told me he was having work done to his other houses and came here looking for somewhere to stay just for a few weeks, while that was in hand. Then before anyone knew it, they were married.' A sly look came over his face. 'All I can say is, how did she draw him in? That's the wonder. That's what gets talked about round here. That's what I told the inspector.'

It took me a moment to realise what he was saying. Miss Una Kenrick, a lady of modest means and blemished beauty, had in a very short time engaged the affections of a gentleman of property and married him. Milton did not know her, of course. He could not appreciate her as a lady of intelligence and character who would be a valued and beloved wife. He could imagine only a devious person whom he suspected had employed an underhand scheme to entrap a rich husband. A husband who was now mysteriously dead.

Our business done, we returned to the Plough, and entered the cobbled yard, a place of noisy industry smelling of stables, burning coals, singed hooves, and hot metal. On enquiring for Mr Empson, we were approached by a man in a heat-burnished apron, wiping blackened fingers on a rag. Despite the cool weather he wore a sweat cloth wound about his neck, which was so saturated it had almost become a part of him.

'What can I do for you, gents?' he asked. He stared at Holmes, then at me, then at Holmes again. 'Are you the men from Barts in London?'

'We are,' said Holmes. 'I have already examined the body of Mr Clark and am seeking further information to assist my investigation. I am speaking to anyone who may have seen or spoken to him recently.'

Empson shrugged. 'I don't know that I can help much. I last spoke to him about three or four weeks ago, about the time he took up residence at Spring Cottage. He came and asked me to put in bolts for the front and back doors.'

'Did he say why he needed them?'

'Only that he thought the existing locks were not secure enough. It's an old house with old fittings, and I don't think Mr Brampton who used to own it did much to improve it. The main trouble is, there's a bit of subsidence at the back, which pulled the rear door out of line. It needs a builder to make it properly good. I told him, I reckon one of the drains is cracked. Could cost quite a bit to put that right, but he said he didn't mind. I mentioned a builder I know, and Clark said if I could give him his address, he would be very grateful.'

'Who was this builder?'

'Oakes, he's an Ilford man.'

'Do you know if Clark saw him?'

'I don't, no.'

'May I have his address?'

This was provided and Holmes wrote it down.

There was nothing more to be learned from Mr Empson, and we thanked him and went indoors to settle in a quiet part of the Plough.

Miss Garbutt brought us a dinner of pea soup with boiled pork and potatoes. 'We'll be very busy soon,' she said. 'Mr Lewis the coroner is coming tomorrow, and we're preparing our upper room for the inquest.'

'I expect we will see the delivery boy who supplied eggs and vegetables to Spring Cottage,' said Holmes. 'His evidence will be very interesting, as he would have been at the house this morning and might have witnessed something important.' He turned to me. 'What was his name again? I have quite forgotten. He draws a little handcart.'

'Oh, that would be Harry Gibson, from Upper Coldwell Farm,' said Miss Garbutt.

'I did not pass the farm on my way from the station,' said Holmes. 'Is it far?'

'No, if you go up the high street and cross over Station Lane, it is hardly ten minutes' walk, Romford way.'

Sarah returned to the kitchen, and we addressed our plain but hearty meal.

'Have you noticed,' said Holmes, 'that all we seem to know about Mr Clark at present is what he has told others? His wife will identify him as her husband, but we are yet to find anyone who has known him longer than a few weeks. Tomorrow, when Mrs Clark has rested, we will see what his papers reveal. And then we may know whether all his precautions were a matter of simple prudence or something else.'

'Holmes,' I said, 'I know that the inspector thought that the hessian was left by the delivery boy, but before he said so, did you have another theory?'

'I did. It seemed to me that the reason for the dearth of boot prints was the fact that a man had approached the cottage with his boots wrapped in hessian cut from a sack. That would explain why there were loose threads. Dry hessian on a clean, dry path would leave almost no marks. A common reason for wrapping footwear in coarse material is warmth, especially if the leather is broken. But it also serves to avoid leaving identifiable prints and muffles the sound of footfall. It is a ploy used by burglars, with whatever common cloth might be available.'

'Hessian will be very common in Coldwell,' I said.

'I fear so.' As he spoke there was a furious rumble from above, quickly followed by a rushing sound like that of a waterfall. 'I hope,' said Holmes, as pounding rainfall battered the windows, 'that Inspector Mackie has taken the hint and looked at the footmarks on the other side of the house, the ones he prevented me from examining and which are now being consigned to oblivion.'

Our dinner done, another man might have spent the evening with a pipe before a warm fire, but Holmes, after observing a break in the weather, determined to return to Spring Cottage to have a further discussion with Mrs Pettigrew. We were obliged to turn up our collars and hurry across the road before it turned too slippery for our feet.

CHAPTER ELEVEN

When Mrs Pettigrew opened the door of Spring Cottage, I could see that she was not especially pleased to see us. She made no move to step aside and allow us to enter.

'Mrs Clark is resting, poor lady,' she said. 'Worn out by all the upset and the questions. You will have to come back tomorrow.'

'Oh, but it is you to whom I wish to speak,' said Holmes, in his mildest voice. 'Kindly allow us in to warm ourselves by the fire, and we will not engage you any longer than need be.'

'Very well,' she said, 'but if I admit you, please promise not to disturb Mrs Clark.'

Holmes made such a charming and humble promise that it would have melted a heart of stone, and we were admitted to the cottage where we made ourselves comfortable in the parlour at the little table. The fire had been dying down, but the housekeeper mended it with a few coals. She remained standing, but Holmes drew out a chair so that she might be seated, and she complied.

'It may be a trivial matter,' said Holmes, stretching out his long legs. He appeared at first glance to be wholly at his ease, but I saw a familiar glint in his eye. 'I ask the question merely to set my mind at rest. I would like to know why several years ago your former employer Mr Brampton cut down the ivy at the back of the house but did not do the same at the front?'

I thought it was a trivial question, but to my surprise Mrs Pettigrew looked discomfited by it. 'Why, what a curious thing to ask!' she said.

'I agree,' said Holmes, casually. 'It was just a strange fancy of mine. Please indulge me. You have said that Miss Brampton slept in the back bedroom, the same room where Mr Clark's body now lies. If I judge the state of the ivy on the back wall correctly, it was cut some five years ago. Is that correct?'

'Yes, I believe it was.'

'And Miss Brampton would then have been what age? Twenty-one?'

'Yes.'

'When I first came here, I saw that a start had been made on removing the ivy at the front of the house. I believe that this must have been done in the last three weeks. Am I correct?'

'Yes. Mr Clark cut the stems himself. He said he would get a man to clear it all away when it had died back.'

'In view of his opinions on securing the property, I can see why he did so, but Mr Brampton's actions were less obvious. I did not know until recently that it was his daughter who slept in that room. I feel somehow that there is a story to tell.'

'There is, but it can have no bearing on Mr and Mrs Clark.'

'Even so, it does interest me, and I would like to know more if only to dismiss it from any consideration.'

Mrs Pettigrew clasped her hands together, in a gesture of indecision. 'Very well,' she said at last, 'I will tell you the truth, Mr Holmes, although I am sorry to say that it is a sad story. Miss Brampton was a quiet, shy young lady, and rather plain. Her only accomplishment was drawing, and that was not sufficient to attract gentlemen callers, at least not the kind of suitors who would meet with her father's approval. I am no judge of these things, but I do recall being told that Miss Brampton had a sour face, and one wouldn't envy the man who saw it across the breakfast table every morning. A cruel way of saying it, but I don't think anyone would deny the fact.

'It was generally known in Coldwell that Miss Brampton was sole heir to her father's estate, although since Mr Brampton was not very elderly, it was supposed she would not inherit for many years. There were rumours as to his worth which unfortunately exaggerated the truth. You see, Mr Brampton's family had once been well-to-do, but through a series of misfortunes they had lost a great deal of their wealth. All they had of value was some heirlooms they could not bear to part with, and that included a set of jewellery which had once belonged to Mr Brampton's mother, and his grandfather's silver watch.'

'The same watch to which Mr Rowe tried to lay claim?'

'The very same. Miss Brampton had no personal fortune of her own, but Mr Brampton promised her that the jewellery would become hers when she reached the age of twenty-one. On her twenty-first birthday, he gave her the jewels in a nice little casket. The result was that several young men suddenly found her more interesting than they had done previously and asked to court her, but it became very apparent to Mr Brampton that they were only interested in her property, and he sent them away.'

'Was your nephew one of those who displayed a change of intention?'

'I don't believe so. He never mentioned it to me or asked me to put in a word for him. I know that Mr Brampton did once catch a persistent suitor at the back of the house, trying to get admission by way of the kitchen. But I am sure it was not Clem. Had it been, I know Mr Brampton would have had words with me about it. The result was that he became concerned that young men might attempt to climb the ivy to Miss Brampton's room and abduct her. Then she would be ruined and be obliged to marry a scoundrel. I don't know how much of a danger that was, but that was what he thought. So he cut it all down. I said to Clem, there will be a great many disappointed young men in Coldwell, now. His reply was that there were plenty of fish in the sea, and he meant to cast his nets wide and see if he could catch a prettier one.'

'Did your nephew ever visit you here?'

Mrs Pettigrew gave a sad shake of the head. 'No, if he came to Coldwell, he was not to be admitted to the house. Not then and not now. I am sorry to say he has a reputation for being untrustworthy. I see him sometimes in Ilford at my sister's when he visits.'

'I believe you said he no longer resides in Essex?'

'Yes, like so many of our young men he decided to make his fortune in London. That was a good many years ago. He comes back from time to time to see his mother and some of his old associates, but I have not seen him for almost a year.'

'So,' said Holmes, 'Mr Brampton cut down the ivy in order to protect a family treasure.'

'I suppose you could put it like that.'

'The question is, was that valued treasure the jewellery or the lady? Which meant more to him?'

'That is a good question. I am not sure I know the answer. But I don't think Mr Brampton ever wanted his daughter to marry. There are fathers, and mothers too, who like to have a spinster daughter in the house and treat her like one of the servants. She was too useful to him. But when Mr Rowe came here to teach, that was about two years ago, he decided to court Miss Brampton — and being of better class than the others, he had a better chance of gaining the father's approval. Mr Rowe called here often, and she sometimes went for walks with him in the company of his sister, Mrs Harmon. But I do not think Miss Brampton cared for him very much. In fact, I know she did not. When he asked for her hand, she rejected him more than once before she finally accepted. She knew she would either marry Mr Rowe or be a spinster, always at her father's beck and call. It was not an easy choice. But accept him she did.'

'Since Miss Brampton's marriage, have there been any attempts at entering the house without invitation, or even forcing an entry?'

'No, nothing of that sort. The jewels were, of course, no longer here.'

'They are now, I assume, in the possession of Mr Rowe?'

'The poor young lady wore them at her wedding. The very next day he sold them and invested the money in a venture he thought would make him rich. He lost every penny.'

'And the silver watch? Where did Mr Brampton keep it?'

'It was locked away in a drawer. He never wore it. I remember Mr Rowe once had a look at it. That was just before he was married. He even asked to take it away and have it valued. Naturally Mr Brampton would not allow it. He said he would see to it himself, but he never did. When Mr Brampton was so very ill, Mr Rowe came here and asked if the watch had been valued. I said it had not. He volunteered his services in that respect, but I told him I would attend to it, and he went away. I did not like or trust his interference. Then the watch passed into the possession of Mrs Clark, and of course her husband.'

'And where did Mr Clark keep it?'

'I'm not sure. Now I come to think of it, I haven't seen it since Mr Brampton died.'

CHAPTER TWELVE

The following morning, a group of men gathered at the Plough. Their serious faces, failed attempts at heartiness, and formal attire suggested that they had been summoned as a coroner's jury. Miss Garbutt, the landlord's daughter, emerged from her labours in the kitchen to greet them and conduct them to a prepared table, where she took their orders.

Holmes and I had already breakfasted on bread, eggs, and coffee, but she took the time to come to us and ask if we required anything else. We thanked her but said we had had sufficient.

'The jurymen like to fortify themselves before they begin,' she said.

'The only gentleman I recognise is Mr Milton,' I said.

'Yes, well, there is Mr Felby from the Old Manor House, the gentleman with white hair; he is well respected and usually acts as foreman. The others are men of business from Romford and Ilford.' At that moment she was summoned to the bar counter by the father and excused herself and hurried away.

'How curious,' said Holmes.

'That seems like a good composition for a jury,' I said.

'It is, but there is a man missing. I wonder why.'

Shortly before the appointed time, Mr Lewis the coroner arrived with his officer and conducted the jurors to Spring Cottage to carry out the solemn duty of viewing the body of the deceased. Once they had returned and further refreshed themselves with Essex ale, they went upstairs to prepare for the hearing.

'Do you think we will be called?' I asked Holmes.

'Not at this stage,' he said. 'But since I am not permitted by the police to question witnesses or look for clues, I must be content with the role of spectator and gather what I can from that.'

Inspector Mackie arrived. He favoured us with a warning look, as if to caution us against interfering, but he was obliged to accept our presence as interested onlookers.

'Well, this is very interesting,' said Mr Danbury, coming to sit with us uninvited. 'Mr Stamford, I would be grateful for an introduction to your associate.'

I obliged him. Holmes gave a curt nod and murmured only those words required by politeness.

'Your arrival created quite a stir in these parts,' said Danbury, 'and I hear you have been very busy. Of course, I know you are prevented by the strictures of your profession from revealing any information about your work here.' He paused to allow Holmes the opportunity of making unwise revelations. After a moment of silence, he continued, 'I have never been to an inquest before. This will be excellent experience for my novel.' If he was expecting us to enquire eagerly as to the subject of his novel, he was disappointed. 'Do you know many people in Coldwell?' he asked. This appeared to be addressed to us both.

'Very few, I am afraid,' I said. 'Mrs Clark is a previous acquaintance, but any others I only met yesterday.'

'Do you see the lady and gentleman sitting apart in the far corner?' he asked, with a little motion of the eyes in that direction.

I turned my head to where he was indicating. 'Yes, who are they?'

'Mr Rowe the schoolmaster and his sister Mrs Harmon.'

I could not avoid a more careful look at the man who had bothered Mrs Clark with his demands, and the lady who had once been a friend of his late wife. The gentleman was aged about forty-five and dressed as was appropriate for the recently widowed. The expression of his features, as far as one might see under a great bush of black beard and brows, matched the sombre garb. His sister, who was about ten years his senior, looked about her with the assured certainty that she was the most notable individual in the room. She was doing her best to ignore the fact that she was in a public bar, having created a little atmosphere of respectability about her to protect her from contact with the common drinker. She too was in mourning, but the colour of her gown, between dark grey and violet, and the white lace collar indicated it was a mark of status rather than grief and was not recent.

'I understand that Mr Harmon is no more,' said Holmes.

'Yes, he died several years ago. He was a payroll clerk in Ilford, but after suspicions arose concerning missing funds, he consoled himself with a glass or two of brandy and accidentally fell upon the railway line, just as the London to Colchester express was passing though.'

'Given the intervals in the timetable, that was singularly bad luck,' said Holmes, drily. 'She wears her grief well.'

'She is not as grand as she pretends to be,' said Danbury. 'Her husband left her impoverished, and she lives off the charity of her brother.'

I could see Holmes beginning to warm a little to the prospect of conversation with Danbury, having observed that his habit of prying made him a useful source of local gossip.

Mrs Clark arrived in the company of Mrs Pettigrew. Both were attired in deep mourning, an article essential to the wardrobe of any lady. Both, I reflected, had had recent occasion to require it. They glanced consolingly at each other but no-one else. To my considerable concern, I saw Mr Rowe rise stiffly from his seat and approach them. The young widow recoiled as he advanced and clutched her companion's arm. Holmes quickly started to his feet in case he was needed, and I followed suit. A few quiet words were spoken by the schoolmaster, and Mrs Clark merely nodded. A cold look from Mrs Pettigrew sent Rowe back to his seat, then seeing us, she led her charge to our table.

'What did that fellow want?' asked Holmes. 'I hope he has not been impolite.'

'Thankfully he only wished to express his condolences,' said Mrs Pettigrew. 'But he need not think he will be allowed in Spring Cottage again or given any property which is not rightfully his.'

Mr Danbury rose to his feet respectfully and bowed as the ladies were seated. I was obliged to introduce him. Once the gentlemen were seated, the aspiring man of letters chatted amiably about his interest in traditional folk tales and how he sought inspiration in them for his writing. It was innocent enough, but I feared he was trying to learn more about Mrs Clark. She remained composed and polite, and revealed nothing.

When the door next opened, it admitted a formally clad gentleman of middle age carrying a leather document case. Mrs Clark greeted him with some relief.

'I came as soon as I could,' he said sympathetically. 'What dreadful news. I promise I shall be of service to you in any way I can.' He was introduced to us as Mr Philpott the solicitor and joined us at the table. Mrs Clark made sure to represent us to him as her trusted associates, while Mr Danbury was introduced rather pointedly as a lodger at the inn.

I would rather have liked Mr Danbury to leave us to our private business, but he did not; indeed I saw him lean forward eagerly in the hope of acquiring more gossip. Mr Philpott, however, recognising the danger, gave him a meaningful stare and observed that he intended to have a confidential conversation with his client and her appointed representatives. Mr Danbury took the hint with regret, rose, bowed, and left us. None of us was pleased to see that he then applied for and received permission to sit at the same table as Mr Rowe and his sister.

'I cannot imagine what Mr Rowe is doing here,' said Philpott. 'This is no business of his.'

'He offered me his condolences,' said Mrs Clark, who did not look the slightest bit pleased to have received them.

'Did he now? Making an effort to undo his previous insults. Well, we will have none of him. I see he has not been admitted to the jury.'

'I observed as much,' said Holmes.

'He was a juror at the inquest on Mr Brampton, which should have been a quickly concluded affair, but instead he took up the valuable time of the coroner demanding to know if his father-in-law had during his illness been capable of making a new will. He made such a fuss the coroner threatened to dismiss him.'

'The insolence!' exclaimed Mrs Pettigrew.

'Did you know, sirs,' Mr Philpott continued, 'that when Mrs Clark inherited the estate of her cousin, that fellow came to me alleging that there had been another will in which he would have inherited everything, and which had been criminally destroyed. I told him there was no such thing and could never have been any such thing. He then attempted to find some fault with the existing will. I told him that it was perfectly in order. Mr Brampton had undoubtedly been careless in making no arrangements in the case of his only legatee predeceasing him, but that did not invalidate the document. Then Mr Rowe claimed that when he married, Mr Brampton promised his daughter that he would give her a silver watch when her first child was christened. This watch is one which was inherited by Mr Brampton from his grandfather. I have not seen it, but I assume it has some value beyond the sentimental. Mr Rowe said he believed this watch was rightfully his. But even if Mr Brampton had made such a promise, there was no witness and no document to prove it. Sadly, the child did not live to be christened, and Mr Brampton was not in a position to make any gifts when his daughter and grandchild died. I told Mr Rowe he had no case and refused to act for him.'

'He came to see me, claiming the watch was his,' said Mrs Clark. 'It was a most unpleasant interview. When I was married, the watch became John's property and I thought that would be the end of it, but he actually accosted John in the street once with the same demand. Of course, John would have nothing to do with him.'

'I fear that before long he will make another attempt on it,' said Holmes.

'Where does Mr Rowe live?' asked Philpott.

'He has rooms, a little apartment at the back of the school, which forms a part of the building,' said Mrs Pettigrew. 'His sister lives with him. I am sure he thinks Spring Cottage much more appropriate to his status.'

Holmes glanced at Danbury, who was deeply engaged in conversation with Mr Rowe. Moments later there were nods on both sides, and Danbury took a card from his pocket and presented it to Rowe. He looked at it, appeared impressed, and put it carefully away. 'Now what is that fellow up to, I wonder?'

'Do you know what his business is?' asked Philpott.

'He claims to be a writer,' I said. There was an embarrassed silence. 'I didn't say he was one.'

At that moment the coroner's officer came down the stairs and addressed us. 'Ladies and gentlemen, please make your way upstairs if you are attending the inquest.'

CHAPTER THIRTEEN

The upper room had been nicely arranged, the best of it being a good fire of coals and logs. There was a large table for the coroner, his papers and the exhibits. The jurymen sat in two ranks on rows of chairs, looking to my mind a lot less queasy than many a jury I had seen in the past. I wondered if any of them had sat at the inquest of the late Mr Harmon.

There was a scant assembly of persons, one of whom, a gentleman with a notebook, I guessed to be a representative of the press.

The gun was displayed on a tray, as were the pair of Persian slippers, one with the hole through the toe, the other complete, as well as the fatal bullet and the rest of the ammunition. I could see that Holmes was extremely frustrated that he had not been able to examine any of these items so far, but he was obliged to swallow his annoyance.

Mr Lewis, his documents arranged tidily before him, announced the opening of the inquest, and called upon the widow to give evidence. His manner was dry and formal, in keeping with the occasion, but he showed creditable kindness to the bereaved. A chair had been provided for the use of witnesses, and Mrs Clark, with an encouraging look from Mrs Pettigrew, stepped forward and took her place. There was a carafe of water and a glass on the table, and Mr Lewis offered to provide her with refreshment, but she declined. A widow is usually accorded considerable sympathy at an inquest on her husband, but as Mrs Clark faced the jury and onlookers, a noticeable chill settled on the proceedings. I recalled what Mr Milton had said about the suspicions attached to her. I could almost sense inquisitive eyes searching her for any signs of guilt.

Mrs Clark avoided the stares of the gathering by directing her attention to her hands, which were folded on her lap. She spoke in a well-modulated voice and gave the same account as she had given us earlier: her husband's demeanour, his usual habits, and his non-appearance at breakfast at the customary hour. She said she had slept soundly that night and heard nothing. There had been no-one else in the cottage apart from herself and the housekeeper.

Mrs Pettigrew was the next to give evidence and described discovering the body and fetching the constable. There had been no visitors on the day prior to Mr Clark's death.

Both witnesses had no hesitation in identifying the body as that of John Clark.

A gentleman was called who announced that he was a dealer in firearms and had previously been consulted by the police in cases involving guns. He had examined the little pistol found at the scene of John Clark's death and had little doubt that it was the one which had made the fatal wound. The calibre of the bullet matched the gun and there were signs that it had been fired very recently. He would describe it as a pocket pistol, of a kind which ladies were known to conceal about them when travelling. There was no trigger guard, and to fire it, one had to first pull back the hammer and then press the trigger. It would not take a great deal of strength to carry out either action.

The most interesting witness was Dr Wright, who began by testifying that John Clark had been in good health. A series of tests were underway to establish whether the deceased was under the influence of alcohol or narcotics or any other poisons, and he hoped to be able to make a full report very shortly. The primary cause of death, however, was the bullet wound to the heart.

He had made a sketch of the path the bullet had taken through the body, which he showed to the coroner and then passed to the jurors for inspection. He was certain that the angle of travel would only have been possible if the deceased had been sitting up in bed when shot, and the gun fired from a position above him.

The coroner asked the crucial question: could Clark have fired the gun himself, or would it have to have been fired by another person? Wright hesitated. 'It is hard to be precise about the distance from which it was fired, especially as the bullet passed through the toe of a slipper. I think Mr Clark might possibly have done so, although it would have been extremely difficult. The deceased was right-handed. A mark of the bullet on the right sleeve showed it was impossible for him to have fired the gun with the finger of his right hand on the trigger. He might have been able to fire it with the finger of his left hand, and either of his thumbs. The question I must ask myself is, are any of these actions at all likely? Why would a man fire at himself from such a curious angle and in such a manner?'

'Might he have been cleaning the gun, or inspecting it, and accidentally fired it?' asked the coroner.

'No, there was not enough light for him to do so. The lamp was unlit and the candle by the bed had not burned down, which it would have done if it had been alight when he died. I am led to the conclusion that the gun was fired by another person. Whether deliberately or by accident, it is impossible to tell.'

Mr Lewis thanked the witnesses and said that he would adjourn the proceedings for two more days for Dr Wright to complete his tests and hoped to conclude the hearing at the next sitting.

As we departed, a messenger boy handed me a telegram. My cousin Lily was due to arrive on the afternoon train.

It was agreed that Mr Philpott, Holmes, and I would repair to Spring Cottage to help Mrs Clark examine her husband's papers. 'Inspector Mackie and a Constable Simmons from Romford have been examining the property to see where an intruder might have got in,' she said. 'And there was another gentleman, a locksmith. They have all been very thorough. Every door, every window, every lock, bolt and catch. It is hard to see how someone might have entered the house making no noise and then left without any sign that they were there. Constable Higgs told me that there were some burglaries in Coldwell several years ago, but the criminals used to enter by forcing windows, which has not been the case here. But it must have been a burglar. I can't think of any other explanation. He must have heard that John was a man of means and imagined that he had brought valuables with him.'

'Did he?

'No, all his property is in his other houses. But now once the police have done their worst, I will have the cottage in my possession again, and may admit whom I please.'

'I am happy to tell you that Lily is on her way,' I said. 'I will meet her at the station and break the news to her before she comes here.'

'Oh, how comforting! Mrs Pettigrew, will you make up a spare bed in my room so Lily can stay by my side?' She sighed. 'Poor John has been coffined now, and the arrangements for a funeral are in hand, but I cannot bury him before Dr Wright tells me I can. I am surprised that no family members have come forward to claim him, as there might already be a burial plot, but I have heard nothing.'

Once we had returned to Spring Cottage, Mrs Pettigrew set about her duties.

'Where did your husband keep his personal effects?' asked Holmes.

'I have his keys here; I think the papers must be in the desk or his trunk. They are all in his room.'

We proceeded to the room in question, which was very cold and dark, the available space dominated by the coffin resting on trestles. The lid was in place but had not yet been fastened down. The drawers of the nightstand had been emptied and the contents arranged on top. They consisted of the usual gentleman's toiletries and pocket handkerchiefs. Holmes opened the drawers and explored them, but there was nothing hidden there.

'You said he wrote letters?' asked Holmes.

'Yes.'

'Where did he post them?'

'I — assume at the post office.' I saw Holmes's eyes narrow at this response and recalled that Mr Milton had told us that John Clark never entered the post office. I thought it best not to query that statement until later, and Holmes, too, said nothing.

'You did not post any for him?'

'No.'

'Did he receive letters?'

Mrs Clark thought carefully. 'I have not seen any delivered. But then we had not been here long. If his friends or business associates sent letters to a former address, then they should have been redirected here, and I suppose that would have delayed them. Although now I think of it, it does seem like rather a long delay. Perhaps they were not redirected after all, and there is a great pile of letters at one of his other houses.'

Mr Philpott was content to stand by and observe as Holmes took the keys and unlocked the little writing desk, which had two flat drawers and some upper compartments for stationery.

The widow sank wearily onto the chair nearby. I thought she was still struggling to believe the dreadful turn of events. 'Is there anything you require?' I asked. 'Should I send for Mrs Pettigrew?'

She shook her head. 'No, I will just rest here. I am so very grateful for your help.' I felt a little guilty at that moment, as I had still to resolve the matter of the letters she had written to Lily. In view of her revelation that all her worries had been resolved, I thought the sooner I retrieved them the better.

Holmes opened the drawers. I glanced into them, but to my surprise they contained nothing but blank sheets of writing paper and pencils, and a leather wallet. He opened the wallet and found twenty gold sovereigns wrapped in a sheet of notepaper and a bundle of currency notes. These he carefully counted under the gaze of Mr Philpott before replacing them in the wallet. Holmes pulled the drawers fully out to examine them, then bent down and peered into the body of the desk. I lit the lamp and brought it close. Holmes pushed his hands deep into the desk, feeling for hidden compartments, then he studied the drawers both inside and out with his glass before replacing them. Mr Philpott, looking surprised, also examined the drawers.

'Have the police searched this desk?' asked Holmes.

'Yes — at least, I gave them the keys.'

'And did they take anything away?'

'No. Mrs Pettigrew watched the search for me and said they looked very disappointed and took nothing away.'

Holmes next made a thorough search of the wardrobe, delving into the pockets of the clothing that hung there, feeling in the linings for anything concealed, then he made a further and more careful search of the nightstand which supplied nothing of interest. There was a small trunk in the bottom of the wardrobe, and he removed it and turned the key in the lock. Underneath some folded linens there was a leather document case, which he lifted out and opened. It contained several sheets of plain brown wrapping paper. Holmes studied them carefully to see if there were any marks or writing, but without result. The search which eliminated the possibility of hidden compartments in the base and lid of the trunk, also yielded nothing. Finally, he examined the interior of the wardrobe, using the lamp for illumination of its surfaces and the top, in case anything had been placed there out of sight. He turned to us and shook his head.

'Mrs Clark, may I see your marriage certificate?' asked Mr Philpott.

'Yes, of course.' She went to fetch it.

We waited anxiously, hoping for enlightenment.

CHAPTER FOURTEEN

It was Philpott who expressed the thought that was already on our minds. 'This is very peculiar,' he said.

'It is extremely peculiar,' agreed Holmes. 'I can understand that a man who is living in lodgings while his properties are being repaired, takes only essential possessions with him, but all he has is clothing, a few toilet articles, from which one item is notably missing, and a supply of money. Not one document. According to Mrs Clark, he wrote letters, but he did not send them, or at least I have been told he did not send them from the post office in Coldwell. The pen and ink have been used, and there was ink on his right forefinger, but we have no trace of anything he wrote. If he made notes on paper, then those papers have been removed or destroyed, and the blotter gives us no clue as to what was written. Where are his papers? What about his bank? Where are these other properties which he says he owns? Who is his agent or solicitor?'

'I have nothing to add,' said Philpott. 'But perhaps the certificate may offer us some insights.'

Mrs Clark returned with the certificate, which showed that she was married by licence in the register office at Romford. Clark gave his full name as John Clark, his age as 50, his rank as 'gentleman', his residence an address in Romford. The certificate also supplied his father's name, which was John Clark and whose profession was also 'gentleman'.

'What address is this?' asked Philpott.

'It is where John was lodging in Romford when we met,' said Mrs Clark. 'But he was not satisfied with the rooms there, which was why he came to Coldwell.'

'Who were the witnesses?'

'They were persons at the register office who agreed to stand as witness for us. We had not met them before.'

'And he would have no certificate of birth,' Holmes observed, 'since they were not introduced until more than ten years after he was born. Do you know the parish of his birth?'

'No, he never told me that.'

'The county?'

'I believe he said he was born in Essex.'

'A pity,' said Holmes, drily. 'I was hoping for Rutland. But I have been told he travelled out of Coldwell on business.'

'He did. And he sometimes went out for walks. I suppose he might have gone to Romford or Ilford; neither are very far.'

'There seem to be no papers at all,' I said. 'Not even a will, which I would have expected. You could be the sole inheritor of your husband's fortune. You might be a very rich woman.' This observation did not appear to bring the widow any comfort.

'Perhaps he deposited his papers with a friend or a solicitor for safety,' she said, weakly. We were silent. There were no clues to lead us to either. And it struck me then that 'John Clark' was such a common name that there might be hundreds of men in England of that name and about the right age.

For a moment, I thought that Mrs Clark would crumple under the strain of her situation and give herself up to helpless tears, but she did not. I saw her gather all her strength and become the quietly determined and courageous lady who had impressed me when we had first met. She took a deep breath, drew herself up straight, and said, 'There might be other papers somewhere in the cottage. If you would give me some time, I will ask Mrs Pettigrew to help me search. And if all else fails, I will place an advertisement in the newspapers. Someone must know the answer.'

'You have told us that your husband planned to go to Wales in the near future,' said Holmes.

'So he told me, yes. He thought he might be away for at least two weeks, perhaps longer.'

'Did he say anything about the location of his properties, the names of the persons he was intending to meet?'

'No, nothing.'

'You said he was taking some items to be valued. Do you know which ones?'

She shook her head. Some tears trembled in her eyes, and she angrily brushed them away. I thought she was annoyed not so much with her deceased husband as the exposure of her own lack of knowledge. 'I will go and speak to Mrs Pettigrew now. She may have some suggestions.' She left the room.

Holmes had a new face of determination about him. He set about the most minute search of the room, at times crawling on his knees, looking underneath furniture, his fingers diving into every small crevice where something, even a tiny slip of paper, might have been concealed. He even lifted the lid of the coffin and diligently searched every item of clothing in which the corpse had been dressed. Mrs Pettigrew had, with the assistance of another lady who regularly carried out this type of duty, laid out the body very nicely. Mr Philpott stared at this remarkable proceeding, but Holmes merely said, 'I have permission to assist with Mrs Clark's documents, which means that I am permitted to do everything in my power to locate them.'

As I watched Holmes at work, admiring his extraordinary thoroughness, a horrid thought crossed my mind, and once it was there, I was unable to dismiss it. I waited for an answer to emerge which would confirm my fears, but Holmes was eventually obliged to admit that there was nothing to be found. 'If he has concealed some papers, they are not in his room or his clothes or on his person,' he said. 'We might tear the whole building apart and find nothing.'

'There must be something,' I said. Holmes did not reply. 'But I have had a thought.' Still no reply, only a raised eyebrow. 'What if "John Clark" is not his real name? In fact, I hardly like to say it, but he might not have been a single man. This marriage could have been bigamous — a sham. He might have another lawful family and that is where his papers are. Poor Miss Kenrick, as I am tempted to think of her now. To be deceived in that way. That explains the proposed journey to Wales. He was going there to spend time with his other family. He has probably told his lawful wife he was coming to Essex on business, and she should not expect him home for some weeks. Those trinkets he claimed he was going to take away to be valued are not even his property. He was nothing more than a thief.'

'It is a plausible theory,' said Holmes, and Mr Philpott agreed.

'By the act of marriage, he has taken possession of Miss Kenrick's property and person,' said the solicitor. 'There are men who prey on women like hunters, professing affection but desiring only their fortunes. I have encountered them all too often. He might have been such a monster. The other consideration that comes to my mind is that even if it should prove to be a lawful marriage — which it would be if he was a single man — if Clark had lied on the certificate, giving a false name, then under the Marriage Act, he is not entitled to any property he hoped to acquire.'

'Mrs Clark may be entangled in a mystery which it would be very hard to solve,' said Holmes. 'But whatever the status of the marriage, she ought to be able to regain possession of the property she inherited from her cousin.' He paused. I wondered if he was thinking the same as I. Property is one thing, but her honour and dignity were gone forever.

When Mrs Clark returned, she said, 'Mrs Pettigrew asked me if we had found the watch, the one Mr Rowe was so eager to have. But it is not here.'

'Do you know where your husband kept it?' asked Holmes.

'I am afraid not. I never saw him wear it. It ought to have been in this room, but he did talk about having it cleaned and valued. He might have taken it to a jeweller. Or I suppose he might have deposited it in a bank for safekeeping. But if he had done so, there should be a certificate to show where it was.'

'I will make enquiries at the banks on your behalf,' said Mr Philpott.

'With your permission, Mrs Clark,' said Holmes, 'I would be happy to make enquiries at the jewellers and watchmakers in this vicinity. I am sorry to say I must also include the pawnbrokers. The post office should have a trade directory I can consult. If any of them hold the watch, they will need to know that the owner is deceased.'

'Yes, I am happy for you to do so, but that is so much trouble, Mr Holmes! I am so very grateful.'

'Think nothing of it,' said Holmes, his nostrils flaring as he scented the intoxicating odour of another mystery. 'It will be my pleasure. Now, the item we seek is a gentleman's silver pocket watch, yes?'

'Yes.'

'Is there anything further you can tell me about it?'

Mrs Clark paused, then said, 'I was making an inventory of the contents of the house before I was married. It must be described on there.' She hurried away and returned very shortly with a cloth-bound exercise book, which she opened to reveal several pages of neat writing arranged in columns. 'Yes, here it is, a gentleman's pocket watch; the maker's name is Jesson and Dene. A slight dent on the outer casing. There were hallmarks, but it was hard to see them exactly. I didn't try to copy them in case I made a mistake.' Holmes looked disappointed. 'There was a mark like a face with whiskers wearing a crown,' she said.

'Ah,' said Holmes, 'the leopard's head, signifying the London assay office.'

'And a lion. The kind one sees on a coat of arms.'

'Silver.'

'And something else I could not make out.'

'Those and the manufacturer's name should be enough to start us on our way. Are there any papers regarding the purchase of this watch?'

She shook her head. 'No. Mr Brampton's grandfather was a surgeon, and he was given it by a grateful patient who was unable to pay his bill.'

'I am sure Mr Rowe would know all the answers,' I said.

'He might, but I have no intention of asking him,' said Holmes.

When Mrs Clark had gone to replace her book, Holmes addressed Mr Philpott and me. 'Let us consider Mr Rowe and his motivation in desiring the watch. It can have no sentimental value for him. I am sure he has other more personal keepsakes relating to his late wife. Therefore, it must have some monetary value, or at least he believes it has. He tried to make an emotional appeal, citing a promise made by his father-in-law, but Mrs Clark was unconvinced. He even resorted to threats, which tells us all we need to know about his character. He then tried the legal approach and failed. I think he must realise that any man who agreed to represent him in court will do so only for payment, even if he believes the chances of success are very small. What is his next ploy? Earlier today, he tried unsuccessfully to make his peace with Mrs Clark, who is single once again, with an estate of some value in her possession, an estate which he once anticipated would come under his control. I do not think Mr Rowe would be prepared to commit cold-blooded murder in order to obtain that estate or any part of it, but I do think he would be prepared to commit cold-blooded marriage.'

With that shocking conclusion, Holmes looked at his watch and turned to me. 'I think you should go and meet your cousin's train.'

CHAPTER FIFTEEN

The weather had brightened, although my mood had not as I waited on the platform for Lily to arrive. She descended from the train with more luggage than anyone else might have thought necessary. I went to help her, and she greeted me warmly. 'Oh, Arthur, I am so pleased to be able to see dear Una at last. I have such a pretty gift for her, and I am longing to see her new home. Is she well?'

'My dear, before we go to Spring Cottage, let us sit and talk a little, as there are some things you must know first.' I saw alarm on her face, and quickly added, 'Your friend is well, and I can also assure you that she has told me that the letters she sent were all due to a misunderstanding which has been settled, so you no longer need to concern yourself about that.'

'Oh, that is such a relief! Was she very angry that I kept them?'

'As to that, all I said was that you had told me you had received some letters as a consequence of which you were worried about her. So she doesn't know that you kept them. In fact, she is feeling rather foolish that she wrote them at all, and I think it is best not to mention them to her.'

Lily was relieved. 'You had better let me have them back, and I will burn them at the first opportunity.'

'I promise I will,' I said, feeling a fresh pang of discomfort at the fact that they were still with the police. 'But come and sit for a moment — there is a waiting room here where I hope we will be out of the wind, as we must talk further.'

The room was damp and smelled of mould. It was obvious that Lily, who was looking troubled again, did not want to remain there any longer than necessary. We seated ourselves on some uncomfortable wooden benches before a fire that was no more than an accumulation of glowing embers.

'I am sorry to have to tell you that when I arrived, I discovered that Mr Clark had passed away the previous night.'

Lily gasped. 'Oh, then I must go to Una at once!' She began to rise from her seat, but I took her hand.

'There is more, and you must hear it first. Please sit down.' Something in my voice and expression must have been enough to make her comply. She fell quite silent and listened attentively. 'The inquest opened this morning. As far as we can gather, there must have been an intruder, quite probably a burglar, and he killed Mr Clark with a gun — the same one Mrs Clark mentioned in her letter. The one hidden in the Persian slipper. The hearing has been adjourned for two days. Mrs Pettigrew the housekeeper is a very sensible person who is looking after your friend, so she is not alone. Her solicitor Mr Philpott has called, and is doing all he can, and Holmes is also here to look into the matter. I have told Mrs Clark that you are coming, and she is looking forward to seeing you again.'

As a mixture of terrible and comforting news, this was a great deal for Lily to appreciate, but I often think she is a great deal more acute than she pretends to be. After a moment or two, she took a deep breath and said, 'Take me to her.'

As we emerged from the waiting room, we encountered Holmes, who had just arrived on the station platform. 'Miss Hargreaves, how good of you to come,' he said. 'I am about to go to Romford on an errand for Mrs Clark.' Lily thanked him, and he bowed and went to wait for his train.

'That is so very kind of Mr Holmes to trouble himself,' she said, as we walked up Station Lane to the high street. I decided to say something merely modest in my friend's praise, as I gathered that she already thought sufficiently highly of him.

Lily was already aware from Mrs Clark's letters that Spring Cottage was in need of repair, but even so she was dismayed when she saw it for the first time. 'And Mr Clark intended to make this into a fine home?' she said. 'It looks about to crumble about our ears!'

Mrs Pettigrew opened the door and was obviously pleased to greet Lily. As we entered, the door of the parlour opened, and Mrs Clark almost flew out into the hallway. There were loud exclamations on both sides as the two young ladies flung their arms about each other like long-lost sisters, then disappeared into the parlour together.

'Best not to disturb them, Mr Stamford,' advised Mrs Pettigrew. 'I shall bring tea and cakes and then leave them alone.'

I wondered if Lily would, despite my comments, reveal that she had given me Mrs Clark's letters, which would lead to some very awkward questions. It then occurred to me that while the ladies were occupied, it might be possible for me to go and recover the letters. Inspector Mackie, I recalled, was lodging at Rose Cottage, one of the terraced houses near the station, the home of Constable Higgs. With the weak excuse that I wanted to inform the constable that Lily had arrived to comfort Mrs Clark, I told Mrs Pettigrew where I was bound, and made my way there.

Although a very small single-fronted house, it had a well-tended appearance, with a pretty little garden at the front and a flower urn by the door, which had once been quite plain but had been nicely painted in bright colours. A young lady was sweeping the path. 'Mrs Higgs?' I asked.

She looked up. 'Yes, what may I do for you?'

'My name is Stamford. I am visiting Mrs Clark, who is a friend of my cousin. Is Inspector Mackie here?'

'He is, yes.'

'I would like to speak to him, if I may. The last time we spoke he told me that if I wanted him, he was to be found here.'

'Come in,' she said. 'He is in the parlour.'

What a difference between this and Spring Cottage, I thought. Mrs Clark's residence, though kept clean and tidy by the housekeeper, showed every sign of lack of care, and a long-standing reluctance or inability on the part of the owner to make improvements or carry out repairs. This humble home reflected the pride of the occupant, with many small but important touches which created a warm sense of welcome as the visitor walked in.

'He's having his tea now,' she said. 'I'll bring another cup and refresh the pot.'

Mackie was seated at a table in one of the smallest and yet most comfortable front parlours I had ever seen, replete with cushions, embroideries, and family pictures.

'Mr Stamford, how might I help you?' he said.

'I thought I should mention that my cousin Lily has come to Coldwell to be a comfort to Mrs Clark in her distress. She will be staying at Spring Cottage.'

'Thank you, it might prove necessary for me to speak to her.'

At this, I couldn't help wondering if the inspector was a married or a single man, as he seemed to be the kind of fellow Lily might find interesting.

'The thing is —' I continued.

His raised eyebrows suggested that he was well aware that my opening words were merely an excuse to come and see him, and he was waiting to hear the real reason. 'Yes?'

'I should also mention that I have spoken to Mrs Clark about the letters she wrote to Lily. The ones I passed to you. She reassured me that it had all been a misunderstanding, and the concerns she expressed were without foundation. So, I was hoping you might return them to me. After all, they can have no bearing on your enquiries.'

'The letters,' said Mackie.

'Yes.'

'You mean the letters in which Mrs Clark described her soon to be late husband's suspicious behaviour, and mentioned the very gun used to kill him.'

'Er, yes,' I said weakly. 'She doesn't know you have them.'

I could see he was rather enjoying my discomfort. 'Mr Stamford, those letters are not your property. I will return them to your cousin when and if I judge it to be appropriate. Now, is there anything else?'

I decided not to say any more in case I found myself in more trouble than I already was. I assured him that I had no further requests, bid him good day, and returned to Spring Cottage.

There were no sounds of weeping or breaking chinaware, so I assumed that Lily had not revealed to Mrs Clark that she had given me the letters. Since Mackie was not there to chase me away, I decided to take a turn around the back of the house, where, as expected, the recent downpour had destroyed any useful footprints. I hoped that Holmes would be permitted to examine the lock on the back door. I gave it a cursory glance but could see no signs of any scratches that suggested it had been tampered with. The door frame was very clearly out of alignment, cracking the mortar, as Mr Empson the blacksmith had noticed when he installed the new bolt. It did not appear to have received the attention of the builder he had mentioned.

Mrs Pettigrew, noticing me through the kitchen window, opened the door. 'May I help you, Mr Stamford?'

'Oh, yes, I am just — admiring your little herb garden.'

'Ah yes,' she said, stepping outside with a smile. 'That was Miss Brampton's favourite place. She used to tend it in all weathers, and she had flowers there, too. You see those markers? One can impress words on them to signify what is planted. Miss Brampton marked them herself, but she used all kinds of fanciful names. She learned them from a little book of herbs and flowers. She left it here when she married, her gift to me. "Look after my garden, won't you?" she asked. I still use the markers, but they are only a decoration. They make me think of her. I don't need to put the proper names of the herbs myself as I know them too well, but hers are still there to appreciate. Some of them are plants that never even grew here. I think they were just her favourites. See this one? Ambrosia. Such a pretty name. White jasmine, fleur de luce, purple bower. She did so love flowers. Perhaps it is because she was named for a flower — Iris. She loved climbing plants, because they signified strength, but the only one that ever flourished here was ivy. She was very upset when her father pulled down the ivy that grew here. I sometimes think — oh, you will think me very foolish — but when I tend the garden, I can feel her spirit still hovering here, happy to see it so well kept.'

CHAPTER SIXTEEN

I waited anxiously for Holmes to return from Romford, and when he did, we repaired to the Plough for a welcome glass of beer and a good dinner.

'The post office provided me with the addresses of a number of watchmakers and two pawnbrokers, all of which I visited,' he told me.

'I assume you have not located the watch?' I said.

'I have not. Neither was there any news which could lead me to it. None of the businesses have either received it or seen anyone resembling Mr Clark making enquiries about it. However, the details supplied by Mrs Clark proved to be extremely useful. The makers, Jesson and Dene, were active only in the latter part of the eighteenth century, and this fits with the use of the crowned leopard assay mark which places the watch as made before 1820. Their watches are extremely rare and highly prized both by collectors and museums, and will command large sums at auction. The most recent sale fetched five-hundred pounds. It is a distinctive item, and we must hope it will not remain hidden for long.

'I was not, however, the first person to make enquiries about such a watch. One of the jewellers recalled a similar approach about a year ago from a man who, like me, only had a description and not the timepiece itself. The man he described bore a strong similarity to Mr Rowe. If Mr Rowe has been coveting this watch for some time, he may well have been making his own enquiries and has learned as much as we know. I also paid a visit to the lodgings where Mr Clark lived before he considered Coldwell. The landlady is a Mrs Young, and she recalled him telling her he was a landowner with properties in Hertfordshire who was travelling the country looking for farms to acquire. It is to her credit that she believed none of it and asked him for payment in advance. I suspect she learned that lesson long ago.'

And now, I thought, Mrs Clark had learned it too.

'I made one other interesting observation,' said Holmes. 'While in the post office I encountered Mr Danbury, who was busy sending letters and telegrams.'

'I was very surprised to see him earlier, hugger-mugger with Mr Rowe,' I said. 'Mr Danbury is a prying nuisance, and I would not imagine that Mr Rowe, for all his frustrations, would want to discuss them with such a man.'

'It was no mere discussion,' said Holmes. 'I observed them, their manner, and their posture. There was business being done. I don't know if it relates to Mr Rowe's intentions towards Mrs Clark, but I mean to find out.' He pushed his empty plate away. 'But the weather has cleared a little, and it is a pleasant evening. I propose we stretch our legs with a walk.'

'As far as Upper Coldwell Farm?' I suggested.

'That may lie on our route. And if it does, we might be obliged to pay a call there out of politeness, and we might even enquire after young Gibson. I would not wish to alarm the inspector with any suggestion that we are on our way to interview one of his witnesses.'

The sky was brighter and for once there was no immediate threat of rain. We soon left the dwellings behind as we followed the old coach road in the direction of the farm. On the way I told Holmes of the discoveries I had made, and my awkward position regarding the letters. He made no comment.

Upper Coldwell Farm was less than half a mile from the Plough. There was a wide gate leading to a yard, where some farm carts were drawn up in a row, one of which, rather smaller than the others, was a hand barrow, the kind normally pulled by a man. Holmes examined it and studied the tracks it had left.

'This must be the cart used to make the deliveries,' he said. 'The wheel tracks are of the right size, and there are recent boot prints.'

As he spoke the farmer emerged from the cottage, not with the friendliest expression. 'And what do you want here, sirs?' he said. 'If you're with the police I have told them all I know, and I don't want to tell it all again.'

'Oh, we are not the police,' said Holmes with a disarming smile. 'We came here to assist Dr Wright in a medical capacity and have just attended the opening of the inquest on Mr Clark. I assume young Master Gibson has already spoken to the inspector, as he made a delivery to Spring Cottage on the morning after Mr Clark's death. Will he give evidence at the next hearing?'

The farmer grunted. 'That's more than I know. Harry has gone up to Romford to see his sweetheart. He went up right after doing the deliveries yesterday and hasn't come back yet. He lodges here and I was expecting him back last night. I had to send one of the hands out with the cart this morning.'

'What is the name of his sweetheart?'

'Mary something, I don't know her second name. He was always so reliable, but once a girl takes his interest, well, you know how it is.'

We both nodded as if we knew.

'Four years or more as my best farm lad, then as soon as he turned eighteen, his eyes were elsewhere.'

'At least he took care to return the cart before he went,' said Holmes. 'I assume he walks to Romford.'

The farmer scratched his head. 'Well, now you say that, I did wonder if he was in a hurry, because he didn't put the cart back where he always does, where it is now. He just put it inside the gate. Yes, he walks up to Romford. I did start to think he might have had an accident of some sort either going or coming back, but there have been wagons up and down that road and they would have found him and brought him back by now.'

Holmes was thoughtful and peered inside the cart, examining the interior with care. 'Did Harry complete all his deliveries?'

'Yes, well, Spring Cottage would be the last one. Then he came back here straight afterwards. He was seen walking up the street with the cart.'

'Eggs and vegetables, I was told.'

'That's right.'

'Forgive my ignorance, as I am a city man, but I am curious as to how these things are managed. How did he carry the eggs in the cart? He must have been careful to avoid breaking them.'

'In baskets on straw. Very careful indeed.'

'And what vegetables would have been in his delivery?'

'Oh, carrots, leeks, parsnips.'

'He would have carried them in sacks, I suppose?'

'No, there are large baskets for the vegetables. They are loaded up at night.'

'But how did he bring the delivery to each customer? I don't suppose he carried the laden baskets to the door?'

'No, he had a scoop. One scoop full is the delivery. The customers leave a bowl or basket outside their doors, and he takes his scoop and fills it up.'

'Ah, I can see that is a good way of managing it,' said Holmes. 'It must be hard work on cold nights, and in wet weather.'

'Oh, well, that's just the way of it,' said the farmer, looking contemptuously at us city men. 'Country folk are used to that.'

'I have heard that a good way of keeping one's feet warm in bad weather is to wrap one's boots in sacking,' said Holmes.

'Is it now?'

'Did Harry Gibson do that? I thought I heard someone say he did. I only mention it because if he did, he would have left no footprints to follow if an accident should have befallen him.'

'I never saw him do that.'

'Oh, then that is my error,' said Holmes.

'I'll tell you who used to do that — it was Bill Cutter,' said the farmer with a laugh. 'Oh, he's long gone now, but he liked to break into houses and creep about stealing whatever he could lay his hands on. And it wasn't done to keep warm. Wrapped his boots in any old cloth he could find so he left no marks for the police. Didn't help him none. Ended up in the county jail, which saw him off.'

'Was he any relation to a Mr Cutter who deals in second-hand furniture?'

'Yes, older brother. I'd not have anything to do with that family if I were you. The son is just as bad. We all know what he likes to get up to, only he hasn't been caught yet. Maybe it was him as did for Mr Clark.' He paused. 'I heard the man was shot dead. Is that right?'

'It would appear so,' said Holmes, carefully, 'although the inquest has yet to return a verdict.'

'Well, if anyone wants a gun round here, Mr Cutter is your man. That's all I'll say.'

The farmer returned to his work, and we turned back to Coldwell village.

'Are you going to make enquiries after Mary in Romford?' I asked.

'I expect the inspector is already doing so, but I fear, I very much fear that Harry Gibson did not arrive there.'

CHAPTER SEVENTEEN

When we returned to the Plough, we found Mr Danbury taking his supper. Once his plate was cleared, he moved it aside, sipped his beer and studied his notebook. Holmes approached his table.

'Mr Danbury, I hope I am not interrupting important business, but I would like a word if you would allow it.'

He looked up at us with a smile and closed the notebook. 'Of course, I am always willing to have a conversation.' We joined him at the table.

Holmes lost no time in addressing the point at issue. 'I believe that although you may one day decide to write for publication, and I wish you every success in that endeavour, it is not currently your main business.'

'And what leads you to that conclusion?'

'I have observed your dealings with Mr Rowe.'

Danbury shrugged. 'I have told you; I am a collector of tales.'

'I have no doubt of that. However, when you handed him one of your cards, you inadvertently left one protruding from your pocket. It is quite distinctive and revealed all to me.'

'Ah,' said Danbury, clapping a hand to his pocket, and finding that the cards were safely housed deep within. He looked puzzled for a moment, then grinned. 'What an artful fellow you are, Mr Holmes. I don't believe you saw a thing!'

'May I?' asked Holmes, holding out his hand.

Danbury chuckled. 'I suppose I had better confess all,' he said, passing a card to Holmes. 'If I don't, I feel sure you will find it out.'

Holmes studied the card and put it in his pocket. 'As I thought. This is a card of Mr Ignatius Pollaky, the well-known detective of Paddington. You are not Mr Pollaky, of course, but I suspect you must be an agent of his.'

'I will not deny it,' said Danbury. 'It is a respectable business, although not everyone sees it that way. When I am conducting an investigation, I find it convenient to pose as an author searching for ideas. Authors will always attract persons eager to tell them their stories, and the more scandalous the better.'

'But I cannot believe you initially came to Coldwell for the purpose of acting for Mr Rowe. I know something of him, and I am wondering if he has just engaged you to look into the question of Mrs Clark's inheritance.'

'I cannot discuss a client's private affairs unless you have any information to share,' said Danbury with a sly look.

'I have nothing to say regarding Mr Rowe.'

'But you are right in one respect. I had other business in this part of the world before I encountered Mr Rowe. I reside in the county and will act for Mr Pollaky on matters relating to this region.' Mr Danbury was in a sociable mood, and we were soon more at our ease. 'I don't mind discussing the business which brought me here, as it is a well-known case that has been widely reported in the newspapers. The Quintinfield mystery.'

'I have read about it,' said Holmes. 'The missing man. Too many crimes to mention.'

'I'm not sure I know of it,' I said.

Mr Danbury proceeded to enlighten me. 'The late Mr Elias Quintinfield was a pawnbroker with a business in Paddington, and he ran that trade for many years about as honestly as such trades ever are. There has never been any accusation against him. His son, Frederick, was his assistant. When Mr

Quintinfield senior passed away about two years ago, the business was left in the sole hands of his son. Frederick, however, was cut from different cloth from his father. He would have been a villain whatever his trade, but as a pawnbroker he was able to conceal criminal activities behind the face of a legal business. He had an ingratiating manner, particularly with ladies who were past the springtime of their lives, and it seems they were generous with gifts to him, which usually took the form of money or jewellery. He actually proposed marriage to two of these ladies, but in both cases the families fortunately got wind of the situation and stepped in and prevented it. When these ladies passed away, their relatives were dismayed to discover that their inheritance was less than they had expected. Some of these families — and I will not name them, of course — chanced to compare their situations with each other, and saw the one thing their deceased relatives had in common: a friendship with Mr Frederick Quintinfield. They made complaints to the police, but without result. If property had been given freely as gifts, it would be hard to prove that a crime had been committed. However, the police did view the gentleman with suspicion, and there were two matters which particularly concerned them. It was believed that the pawnshop, while outwardly respectable, was conducting a trade in stolen goods. Also, there was a rumour that the death of Mr Quintinfield senior had not been a natural one. About six months ago, just as it seemed that the police would question Mr Frederick and even exhume the body of his father, he suddenly vanished. I say "suddenly", as one of his assistants said his employer had received a note which alarmed him so much that he left the premises immediately. He did not even have time to clear his bank accounts — or perhaps he realised they might be watched, and he would be arrested if he appeared at the bank. He has not been seen since. I understand that the banks have been alerted to inform the police at once if he tries to withdraw his funds, which are substantial. There is one other curious thing. Mr Quintinfield senior died intestate. The son, although sole heir, had not gone to probate. I know that some people tend to put off these tiresome legal matters. But it does mean that the missing man has no access to either his own accumulated wealth or his father's estate.'

'And you have come here in search of him?' I asked.

'I have. Until recently it has been assumed that he has been in hiding with one of his criminal associates, quite possibly still in London, and waiting for the opportunity to lay his hands on his ill-gotten gains. Recently, however, a grandson of one of the ladies Quintinfield had courted was visiting friends in this county and saw a gentleman's ring offered for sale in the window of a jeweller's shop. On examining it, he was in no doubt that it was a ring that had once been the property of his late grandfather, which his grandmother had gifted to Mr Quintinfield. Enquiries were made, but all that could be discovered was that it had been sold for cash by someone who was not known to the shopkeeper. A lady, I believe. But she may have been acting for the seller. She did not give a name. Mr Pollaky had been approached by the families of the deceased ladies and as it seemed that Mr Quintinfield might be in Essex, I was asked to look into it. If he was here, he would have arrived at some time in the last six months, and through careful questioning I was able to identify some suitable suspects. All of them I have been able to exclude from my enquiries. In fact, one of these was the late Mr Clark. He was a hard man to make a casual acquaintanceship with, as he did not frequent the local shops or hostelries. I did eventually encounter him on a train, and briefly passed the time of day with him.'

'What journey was this?' asked Holmes.

'It was only a few days before his death. I was travelling up to Manor Park, as I had received information that the man I wanted might be there, but it came to nothing.'

'Did you discover where he was bound, and his business?'

'He was very reserved, and I didn't press him. He alighted at Ilford. But I was able to observe him and was satisfied he did not meet the description of the man I sought.'

'Let us know your description,' said Holmes.

Danbury hesitated.

'I promise I will advise you should I see a suspect character of that appearance,' said Holmes.

Danbury smiled. 'It is not especially helpful. He is of medium height. Dark beard and hair, and he is thirty-seven years of age. No distinguishing marks. Sadly, my enquiries have yielded no result. I fear he must simply have been passing through the region, and I will say so in my report.'

'His history?'

'Born in Paddington, never married as far as we know. But —' and here Danbury uttered a sigh of regret — 'I have the feeling that I am looking in the wrong place. Mr Pollaky discovered a man who knew Quintinfield as a youth and said he had a weak constitution and was of melancholy disposition. Perhaps, once he knew the police were on his track and a life in prison lay ahead of him, he made his escape in a more permanent manner. I don't know. He is a slippery type. He's disappeared before. When he was twenty, he suddenly went away, and the father wouldn't or couldn't say where he was. Then some years later he turned up like the prodigal son. The father welcomed him back with open arms and took him into the business again. There were all sorts of rumours, of course. Some said the son had run away to sea, some said he had been in prison, some said he had gone to make his fortune in America, lost all his money and come back.'

Holmes was thoughtful and said nothing.

'I suppose the jewellery might have passed through several hands before it came to these parts,' I said. 'It will be a hard trail to follow.'

'But I must continue my search for as long as I am directed, in order to earn my crusts,' said Danbury, 'and there is a reward for his capture, too. The relatives of the deluded ladies have clubbed up a nice little sum.'

Holmes, as I am sure my readers are aware, was not a mercenary man. In the years of his fame, he often declined commissions which would have brought him great wealth, either because they were of no interest, or he did not care for the character or motives of the person who had approached him. As a student of modest means, however, the prospect of a reward added a significant relish to an already intriguing mystery. Mr Danbury could not have been aware that his enquiry had captured the interest of the finest detective of this or indeed any age.

'I assume the reward is for the capture and conviction of the fugitive?' said Holmes.

'Yes, I am afraid his decaying corpse would not answer.' Mr Danbury swallowed the rest of his drink and rose from the table. 'And now, I must once more seek out this cold trail and hope for victory, but I fear it will lead only to a grave.'

As the disappointed detective left us, I commented, 'Mr Danbury was rather eager to suggest to us that his quarry was deceased.'

'And careful to supply us with no details of the clues he has been following, and a description which could apply to thousands of men. But he did reveal something of significance. Mr Quintinfield's curious and lengthy absence from his father's business. People tend to go for safety to those places which are familiar to them. If it was possible to discover where he had been during that time, perhaps living under another name, or involved in another venture, it would be the very first place I would look.'

CHAPTER EIGHTEEN

There was an almost tangible anticipation in the Plough when the next hearing of the inquest was opened. Something was in the air, as if monumental events were about to happen. Holmes observed drily that village gossip had been hard at work. If Mr Danbury really had been collecting ideas for a novel, he would by now have accumulated enough for a three-volume set. The detective was there as I expected and appeared quite unable to contain his delight. 'I think that he has had a hand in the matter, and knows more than we do,' said Holmes. Mr Rowe also arrived early, and his expression was as solid as stone.

'Note the remarkable communication between Mr Danbury and Mr Rowe,' said Holmes, as the two men sat well apart.

'They are not so much as looking at each other, let alone speaking,' I said.

'Precisely,' said Holmes.

Inspector Mackie attended accompanied by Constable Simmons. He glanced in our direction and said nothing. Mrs Clark, Mrs Pettigrew, and Lily crept quietly in, and I was pleased to see that Mr Philpott was with them. The room became more crowded by the minute. I didn't know the number of the adult population of Coldwell, but it seemed as if every man and woman in the village wanted to be there. Well before the resumed inquest was due to commence, every seat was taken. Those individuals who did not obtain one, were obliged to stand and stare angrily at those who had. Some resorted to sharing a place, squeezing two persons onto a chair meant for one, and a few even attempted to crowd into the area reserved for members of the jury and were told to desist by the coroner's officer. An effort was made to clear the inquisitive from occupying the staircase, but they only moved away briefly before coming back again. I saw messages being passed back and forth along the human telegraph line between those at the top who were able to observe the proceedings and the assembly of no less interested persons who were fated to stand in the street.

When some semblance of order was achieved, and Mr Lewis and the jury were in their proper places, the hearing commenced. The coroner began by presenting the facts which had been established at the first gathering and advised the jury that they were entitled to bring a verdict not only on the cause of Mr Clark's death, but also whether this was due to misadventure, suicide, manslaughter, or murder. If the two latter, they might if they wished name the individual or individuals they believed to be responsible. If they felt there was insufficient evidence for a firm decision, then they should return an open verdict.

The first witness was Dr Wright, who said that he had completed all his tests. The deceased had been in sound health for a man of his age and was not under the influence of drink or any soporifics or medication. The cause of death was a single gunshot wound to the heart. Having considered all the circumstances very carefully, he did not think the man could have shot himself by accident, neither did he think that he had taken his own life. The direction of the wound and the fact that the gun had not been discharged close to the body indicated that he must have been shot by another person. Whether this was done deliberately or by accident, it was impossible to determine.

Mrs Pettigrew was the next witness. She told the court that the gun and the Persian slippers were Mr Clark's property, and he used to keep them in the top drawer of the nightstand beside his bed. She had not been aware that the gun was loaded. On the night of her employer's death, she had locked and bolted the front and back doors at ten o'clock as usual, shortly after he had gone to his bedroom. She had retired for the night about half an hour later. Mrs Clark had retired to her room at about the same time. She did not admit anyone to the house on that day either before or after that hour. She had slept soundly and had not heard a gunshot. She did not leave her room until early the next morning.

'Do you ever admit relatives of yours to the cottage?' asked the coroner suddenly.

'I have never admitted any relative of mine to the cottage. I do not receive personal visitors.'

The coroner nodded, satisfied. I saw Mr Danbury chew his lip.

A gentleman who was unknown to us stepped up. He was formally dressed, with an assured bearing. 'My name is James North, and I am a locksmith. My business is in Chelmsford. I have many years' experience of advising the police concerning burglaries. In my opinion, a lock has not been made which cannot be opened with skill, the proper tools, and enough time. In practice, however, it is rare to find a burglar who has all three.'

'If a lock has been opened,' said the coroner, 'that is, by someone who does not have a key and attempts unlawful entry, will that leave signs to show what has occurred?'

'It will be obvious to the expert eye. In the case of Spring Cottage, I was able to examine all the locks in the house. I was satisfied that entry had not been made through a window.

Concerning the doors, there is another factor, of course — the bolts which were installed by the deceased. Any intruder intending to enter by either the front or the back door would have to open both the lock and bolt. It is more likely that an attempt would be made on the back door, where the intruder was less likely to be noticed. I have made a careful examination of both door locks and there are no signs on either to suggest that they have been opened using a lock pick. The opening and closing of those locks has only been effected by use of a key.'

'Can a bolt be operated from the exterior?' asked the coroner.

'It can. I have seen a burglary in which the criminal drilled a hole through the mortar surrounding the door frame, allowing access with a tool which enabled him to slide the bolt. On leaving the premises he used a loop of cord, the ends of which he had drawn through the hole he had made, to pull the bolt back in place from the outside. He then removed the cord and filled the hole with some material he had brought with him. To the casual observer, it appeared quite untouched. In the case of Spring Cottage, I could discover no evidence that the front door bolt had been disturbed. The back door was another matter. There is subsidence at the rear of the house which has distorted the door frame. It has been in that state for some time and requires urgent attention. A crack has opened in the mortar which I am sorry to say is an open door to an experienced burglar. My conclusion is that it is not impossible for there to have been an intruder, but if all had been secured as we have been told, such a person would have needed to use a key as well as skill in manoeuvring the bolt, or to have been admitted by a person inside the house. Alternatively, the door might have been left unlocked and possibly also unbolted either through negligence or deliberately.'

The coroner recalled Mrs Pettigrew, who was deeply offended by the suggestion of negligence and remained adamant that both front and back doors had been locked and bolted on the night of Mr Clark's death. The only persons who had keys to those doors were Mr and Mrs Clark and herself, and she could not imagine why anyone would want to admit a stranger to the house at night.

Inspector Mackie was next to give evidence. He said that the police had examined the property and discovered no compelling evidence that an intruder had effected an entry on the night of the murder. The windows were fastened and untampered with. It was not possible to climb in either by the ivy, which had been cut, or the drainpipes, which would not have held the weight of a person. His opinion, after hearing the evidence of Mr North, was that anyone entering Spring Cottage must have been admitted by someone in the house who drew the bolt and then unlocked the door. He believed that Clark was shot either by someone already in the house or someone admitted by a person in the house.

'Did the police carry out any tests to establish whether it was possible for a gun to be fired in the back bedroom though something like a slipper, without waking the other residents of the house?'

'We did. The gun was discharged through a cushion. The report could be heard by persons placed in both upper- and ground-floor bedrooms, although whether it would have awoken a sleeper would depend on the depth of sleep.'

'Have you in your searches of the house discovered anything which might cast any light on a possible motive for the crime?' asked the coroner.

'I am afraid not. We have been extremely thorough and have found nothing that suggests any reason for the crime. We were surprised by the complete lack of any documents. There is nothing to show who John Clark was or where his property might be.'

'Is it possible,' said the coroner, 'that Clark might not be his real name?'

'That is a possibility which must be considered, yes.' A ripple of murmuring ran about the room and the coroner called for silence.

At this point, one of the jurors rose to his feet and politely cleared his throat. 'Excuse me, gentlemen, but I am able to confirm the man's identity. I had no idea until this moment that it was in any doubt. I knew him many years ago but recognised him at once when I saw the body.'

The ripple became a significant stir, which quickly extinguished itself as everyone fell silent, wanting to hear more.

'Please state your name,' said the coroner.

'Harold Forbright. I am an ironmonger with businesses in Romford and Ilford.'

'This is extremely unusual, but please step forward and give your evidence to the court.'

Mr Forbright obliged. He was a stout, comfortable-looking gentleman of middle age. 'When I was a young man, I worked as an assistant to Mr Clark's father, who was a dealer in hardware with a premises in Ilford. The deceased also worked there.'

'When did you last see him?'

'Very many years ago. Maybe twenty.'

Mr Lewis looked doubtful. 'And are you quite sure of the identification? A man may change a great deal in that time.'

'Quite sure, yes. I knew it was him at once when I went to view the body. There is a chipped tooth and a scar on the upper lip which he tried to cover with a heavy moustache. But I looked for it, and there it was.'

'I see. What do you know of Mr Clark's family?'

'His father was a widower. He died about five or six years ago. There were no brothers or sisters, at least, none living, only an uncle — the late mother's brother, but he left Ilford a long time ago.'

'Was Mr Clark married when you knew him?'

'He was single then. I never heard he had married.'

The coroner thanked Forbright, who sat down.

Lewis called his next witness, Mrs Una Clark.

Mrs Clark rose from her seat, steadying herself for the ordeal, and as she did so I saw Lily press her hand with a smile of encouragement. The widow walked to the witnesses' chair at the front of the room. When offered a glass of water, she thanked the coroner and said she did not require it. I thought she wanted the questioning to be over as soon as possible.

The initial questions were straightforward. Her recall of the night in question was the same as Mrs Pettigrew's. She had retired to her bed not long after her husband. She had slept well and heard nothing. She did not admit anyone to the house and did not leave her room until the morning.

'What knowledge do you have of your late husband's wealth?' asked the coroner.

'I only know what he told me, that he had private funds and owned a number of properties.'

'Where are these funds held? And where are the properties?'

'I am sorry, but I don't know. He mentioned Wales, that is all.'

'He did not show you any papers relating to his wealth?'

'No. I have appointed a solicitor, Mr Philpott, to look into those matters for me.'

'You must have expected when you married that you would be a wealthy woman on your husband's death.'

'I did not give that any thought. I thought only of the pleasant life we would have together.'

'Do you know of any will?'

'No.'

'Did he ever discuss making a will?'

'No.'

'Did your late husband have any relatives who might make a claim on his property if he died intestate?'

'I don't know. He never mentioned any. I had the impression he had no living family.'

The coroner paused and after a little cough, opened a folder of documents before him. 'Mrs Clark, I know this must pain you, but these matters must be aired. What was your relationship with your husband? Was he kind, affectionate? Did he confide his feelings and concerns to you?'

'He was very kind,' said Mrs Clark, firmly. 'I know he did not tell me everything about himself, we had not known each other long, but I am sure he would have revealed more in time.'

'But you were concerned about his secrecy, were you not? Did you distrust him? In fact — I must be blunt, were you afraid of him?'

The witness appeared shocked by the question. 'I — no, not at all.'

Mr Lewis sighed and showed her one of the documents in his folder. As he held it up to her view, I knew at once exactly what it was. At that moment I would have liked the floor beneath my feet to gape open so I could disappear through it, never to be seen again. 'Mrs Clark,' said the coroner, 'did you write this letter?'

CHAPTER NINETEEN

The witness gasped and uttered a cry. 'Where — how —?'

'Never mind that. I want to know if you wrote this letter to Miss Lily Hargreaves.'

'Lily!' exclaimed Mrs Clark, staring accusingly at her friend.

To my horror, my cousin turned to look at me and cried, 'Arthur, what have you done?'

There was consternation in court, everyone talked excitedly to everyone else, and the news rippled like wildfire across the room, tumbled down the stairs and surged out to the crowds below. The only person lacking the power of speech was myself.

'May we have some quiet in the court, please,' said Lewis. It was some time before order was restored and the case could be resumed. 'Mrs Clark, I must ask this question again, and it is the only one with which you must presently concern yourself. Did you write this letter?'

The poor woman, clearly in great distress, nodded.

'Thank you. In this letter you express your concern about your husband's secretive behaviour, his long walks from which he returns with muddy, damaged clothing, the strange smells about his person. You hint at darker secrets which you cannot bring yourself to commit to writing. You beg your friend not to send letters to you at Spring Cottage but to the Coldwell post office addressed to another name entirely, left to be called for. Who is Jane Dalton?'

'That is my mother's maiden name,' whispered Mrs Clark.

'Why did you ask your friend to write to you at the post office addressing the letters to your mother's maiden name?'

'It — seemed like the right thing to do.'

'Were you concerned that your husband would open your letters?'

'No.'

'Then please explain yourself.'

The unhappy woman wiped her eyes. The coroner signalled to his officer, who provided her with a glass of water. This time, she took the drink gratefully, and after some moments was recovered enough to speak. 'Coldwell is a very quiet, almost lonely place,' she said. 'When I inherited Spring Cottage I had not expected to live here, but when I met John, everything happened so fast, and here I am. I am not sure I knew what to expect, but after my old life in London I began to feel bereft of my usual amusements. I like to read and thought I might try to compose a story, but I was not confident that I could make it interesting or describe a drama which a reader might find convincing. So — I began to write and somehow, it took the form of letters — and then I don't know why, I thought of sending them to Lily to see what she thought. Just a few and then I was going to write to her to say that all was well, and I had made a silly mistake. Then I would invite her here and we would have such a jolly time, and I felt sure she would forgive me.'

For a few moments there was silence in the room, then the inevitable hum of whispered conversation, which included some laughter. Mr Lewis ordered the noise to cease. 'Mrs Clark,' he began, 'am I to understand that you are claiming that what you have written in these last three letters is made up?'

'Yes.'

Lewis re-examined the letters. 'But you refer to the gun hidden in the Persian slipper.'

'Yes, I thought that might make the story sound more interesting. I didn't know it was loaded.'

'So the direction to the post office, the false name, the demand that your friend burn the letters, that was all to create a drama?'

'Yes. I am sorry. I really am. I don't know how they came to you. They should never have seen the light of day. I told Lily to burn them.'

'Because you were ashamed of them? Because they were a fiction? Or perhaps because they were true?'

'They are not true,' pleaded the author, but I feared that the damage had been done. Even if the jury accepted that the contents of the letters was a fiction, it was proof, especially to men who did not know Mrs Clark, that she was adept at telling convincing lies.

Lewis put the letters back in his folder and removed another paper, an official-looking document. As he did so, I saw a sudden movement, that of Mr Danbury leaning forward in his seat. 'I have one more question to clarify, Mrs Clark. It has been alleged very recently that this is not the first time you have been in a house where there was an unusual death.'

'Unusual?'

'The death of your former employer, Mr Jeffs. I have here the papers regarding the interview you gave to the police on that occasion. You were Miss Kenrick then?'

'I was Mr Jeffs' housekeeper. He was eighty-eight years of age and unsteady on his feet. He was often quite stubborn about being assisted to walk and he fell down the stairs.'

'His relatives made some accusations against you, as a result of which you were questioned.'

'They had neglected him, and they felt guilty.'

'He gave you money.'

'He gave me a five-pound note.'

'There were allegations of missing jewellery.'

'The relatives squabbled over his legacy. There was a gold chain that three of them wanted. One of them must have taken it and blamed it on me. Those papers will show that I was not charged with any crime.'

Mr Lewis had no more to say, and Mrs Clark was allowed to return to her seat. The revelations about her former employer were news to me, but I remained confident that they were of no importance in the case.

'Is that all the witnesses?' asked Lewis. 'Inspector Mackie, you said there was a witness you wished to present.'

Mackie rose. 'I was hoping to locate a Harry Gibson, who made a delivery of eggs and vegetables from Upper Coldwell Farm to Spring Cottage on the day of Mr Clark's death, but he appears to have gone to Romford and it has not been possible to locate him. If anyone here has seen him, I would like them to come forward.'

'Is he a suspect in this case?'

'Not at present, no, although I am unable to rule it out. But I have no evidence to suggest that he ever entered the house.'

'Very well, I think I can now ask the jury to consider a verdict.' Mackie sat down and Mr Lewis made a final ordering of his papers. 'Gentlemen, you must consider first of all the cause of Mr Clark's death. I think the evidence given by Dr Wright is very clear, that this was the gunshot wound to the heart, and I do not expect you to find otherwise. Dr Wright has also stated that the shot must have been inflicted by another person. Whether that was done with the intent of killing Mr Clark or by accident is something you will wish to consider. The other two residents of the cottage deny any involvement in the death of Mr Clark. They also deny allowing another person to enter the house, either deliberately or through negligence, yet we have been unable to show how anyone else could have entered the house without the connivance of one or both. Even if there was an accomplice, it is not hard to imagine that the principal director in what occurred was one of the other residents.'

He paused and went on. 'Mrs Pettigrew is well known to you. She was a trusted employee of Mr Brampton for many years and nursed him assiduously during his final illness, with no thought or expectation of receiving anything other than her usual wages. Mrs Clark, however, is a lady you hardly know. Leaving aside any concerns about the death of Mr Jeffs in which she must in the absence of any evidence to the contrary be considered wholly blameless, we know that she was not a lady of great fortune before she met Mr Clark. We also know that he had told her he was a man of property, the owner of several houses. The letters she wrote to her friend Miss Hargreaves show her to be either a woman in fear of her new husband, or a creator of fanciful stories, or perhaps both. We may never arrive at the truth of that.

'Your choices are clear. Was Mr Clark's death due to misadventure? Was it a manslaughter, an illegal act which resulted in an unintended death? Or was it murder? Do you wish to retire to consider your verdict?'

The jurors, faced with a difficult decision, agreed that they wished to retire to another room to debate in private. They filed out. 'You will be called to hear the verdict in due course,' said Lewis.

'Might I suggest,' said Holmes, to our little party, 'that we repair downstairs, where a fortifying stimulant might be in order?' No-one dissented. I was unable to say a word as we walked down the stairs, pushing my way past the waiting crowds, some of whom were now seated on the steps, my legs having lost most of their power to hold me up. I could not look any of my companions in the face and dreaded the inevitable conversation which would follow. I must have looked like a haunted man.

We found a table in a corner, and Holmes ordered what was required. Mrs Clark was understandably distraught and clung to the arm of Mrs Pettigrew while being supported by Mr Philpott. These, I realised sadly, were now the only persons she felt she could trust. Assailed by a series of betrayals, she was struggling to appreciate what had occurred.

'Una,' whispered Lily, 'I am so sorry. I know you asked me to burn the letters, but I was worried about you and had to consult someone.'

'Was it you who gave them to the coroner?' asked Mrs Clark.

'No! I would never do such a thing!'

It was time for me to confess. 'Lily gave them to me,' I said. 'When she showed me the letters, it was obvious that she was deeply concerned for you. Since you had told her not to come to Coldwell, I offered to come and see you and find out if you were well and safe. I wanted to discuss the letters with you and brought them with me. But when I arrived — it was the morning after your husband's death. At that time, I had no knowledge at all about what had happened. I was questioned by the inspector, and he demanded to know why I had come. I mentioned our worries about you and to support what I had said, I showed him the letters. I asked for them back, but he said he had to keep them. I suppose it was he who gave them to the coroner.'

'And the papers about poor Mr Jeffs?'

'I know nothing about that,' I said.

Holmes had returned to the table and Mr Garbutt brought us some glasses, a jug of beer and another of brandy and water, which were very welcome.

'I have little doubt as to whose diligent efforts exposed those papers and passed the information to the court,' said Holmes. 'Mr Danbury has been employed by Mr Rowe to discover anything to the detriment of Mrs Clark and came up with this unfortunate episode.'

'For what purpose?' exclaimed Mrs Pettigrew, as she poured our drinks.

'Either to have Mrs Clark convicted of murder so she was unable to inherit her husband's estate, which would strengthen his legal claim on the watch, or, if her record was shown to be spotless, he would offer marriage in order to acquire the estate.'

'The villain!' said Mrs Pettigrew. No-one dissented.

'I would not marry that man for the greatest fortune in the world,' said Mrs Clark.

'I am pleased hear it,' said Mr Philpott. 'Be assured he will never succeed in any campaign to claim your property.'

Mrs Clark, looking calmer and more thoughtful, made short work of her brandy and water. 'I see it now,' she said. 'I have been very foolish. In fact, the reason those silly letters are now being held against me is not because Lily didn't burn them, and not because she showed them to Mr Stamford, and not because he came here with them and was obliged to give them to the inspector. No-one has acted wrongly except me. It is I who am to blame for writing them in the first place.'

'Holmes, I did think when you first saw the letters you deduced there was nothing to be concerned about,' I said.

Holmes sipped his beer. 'Handwriting often reveals emotion,' he said. 'Excitement, grief, fear, these will create an unusual flow of the pen, which is why I asked to see other letters for comparison. Mrs Clark has a clear, steady hand. When she wrote about her good fortune, there were signs of increased speed of writing; but when she wrote of her anxiety, her hand was as firm and calm as normal. I would mention it to Inspector Mackie, but I doubt that he would be inclined to take my advice.'

I could only agree. I did not know it then, but one day there would be policemen who would value Holmes's opinion, and seek him out for a consultation; however, those days had not yet come. Only Lestrade, unimaginative, plodding Lestrade, who was then a mere sergeant, had come to appreciate the genius of Sherlock Holmes, if only because he had achieved good results after following his advice.

'What do you think the jury will decide?' asked Lily. 'I mean, they have to see that the letters don't prove anything.'

'We can do nothing but wait and see,' said Mr Philpott, but he did not look confident. Unexpectedly, Lily burst into tears. I saw Mrs Clark gaze at her sympathetically and reach out and squeeze her hand, which only made her cry harder.

Holmes took the opportunity to ask the solicitor if his enquiries at the nearby banks had borne any fruit, but was told that they had not. None of the banks had ever seen Mr Clark. He had no account with them and neither had he deposited any valuables.

After what seemed an age, we were summoned back to the court, where the jury confirmed that they had succeeded in reaching a verdict. The foreman rose to his feet, and his expression was enough to strike dread. 'We the jury unanimously find that Mr John Clark died as a result of a gunshot wound. We also find that he was murdered either by or at the instigation of Mrs Una Clark. We attach no blame to Mrs Pettigrew.'

There was an immediate scramble for the exit by members of the press, forcing their way through the crowds, and excited shouts echoing across the room. Some even put their heads out of the windows and shouted the news to those waiting below. Lily flung her arms about her friend and seemed to be more in need of comforting than the accused.

It took some time to restore calm, then Mr Lewis thanked the jury and nodded to Inspector Mackie, who approached us. Mrs Clark remained seated, but she knew what was to follow. 'Mrs Una Clark, I am arresting you on suspicion of the murder of your husband John Clark.' The usual caution followed, but I am not sure she paid it any attention.

'Am I to be put in irons?' she asked drily.

'Not at all. I shall ask Constable Simmons to convey you to Romford, where you will be accommodated at the Old Court House. I will be along to interview you fully a little later today.'

'It's a disgrace!' exclaimed Lily. 'Una would never hurt a fly.'

Mrs Clark patted her arm and allowed herself to be led away. Mr Philpott was permitted to accompany her.

'And now, Mr Stamford, before I return to Romford, I would like to have a little talk with you,' said the inspector.

'With me?' I exclaimed.

'That's right. Let us go back to Rose Cottage, and we can talk about where you were on the night of Mr Clark's murder.'

That was when it struck me. There had been mention of Mrs Clark directing the actions of an accomplice. I had no alibi for that night, and Inspector Mackie suspected that I was the accomplice.

CHAPTER TWENTY

I looked around for Mr Philpott, but by then he had already departed with Mrs Clark.

'Am I being accused of anything?' I asked.

Mackie grinned. 'Oh, this is just a friendly chat.'

'I will accompany him,' said Holmes.

'Are you his representative?' asked Mackie.

'I am his friend.' I am sure any reader of my memoirs will appreciate that it was worth being under suspicion of murder to hear Holmes say that.

Inspector Mackie looked at us, glancing from one to the other, his eyes narrowed as if judging us, then he grunted. 'Very well.'

Mrs Pettigrew took Lily, who remained visibly distressed, back to Spring Cottage while we accompanied the inspector. As we left the Plough we saw members of the jury, their duty done, placing orders for hot meals and beer. The smells from the kitchen might have whetted the appetite of a statue, but mine had vanished.

'Don't say anything unless asked,' Holmes instructed me quietly as we walked up to Rose Cottage. He must have thought my nerves would make me blurt out something I would later regret, and on consideration I thought he was probably correct.

Seated once more in the warm little parlour, the inspector began. I still thought that he was about to arrest me, but he did not, although I feared that I was a hair's breadth away from such a fate. I wondered what the cells were like at Romford police station.

'I want to understand your involvement in this business,' said Mackie. 'You, Mr Holmes, have a witness to your location at the time of the murder. I have made enquiries at Barts, and it can be confirmed that at the probable time of Mr Clark's death you were in the chemistry laboratory working very late. You may be in trouble with the warden when you return, as there are some recent burn marks on a bench there, but that is not my concern. Mr Stamford, I would like you to begin at the beginning, and tell me what events resulted in your coming to Coldwell.'

Holmes asked for me to be supplied with a glass of water, and while this was being provided, I tried to order my thoughts. After a calming draught I opened my account with Lily's visit, her obvious concern, her revealing to me the recent change in her friend's fortunes and the contents of her letters. I thought that I could be of service to both ladies by going to Coldwell. Either I might be able to render assistance to Mrs Clark, or, if that did not prove to be necessary, I could reassure my cousin that all was well. I emphasised that I had no notion of the tragedy that had taken place until I arrived. From the corner of my eye, I saw Holmes listening to my words with the occasional nod of approval.

'Your landlady states that she did not see you at all between the morning of the day of your cousin's visit and the following morning, when you left for the railway station,' said Mackie. 'She recalls your cousin's arrival and her later departure. Mr Holmes was also there but left before your cousin. You have told me that you remained in your lodgings until the next day, when you went to take the morning train. But there are no witnesses to support your statement. In fact, having examined the timetables of the trains from Liverpool Street, I can see that there was more than enough time for you to travel to

Coldwell that very same night, shortly after your cousin left. The stationmaster at Coldwell recalls a passenger, a gentleman, alighting late that evening, but unfortunately could not identify him. Now supposing, Mr Stamford, in order to be of service to your cousin, with whom you are on very affectionate terms, you decided to go to Spring Cottage, where Mrs Clark, who was already an acquaintance of yours, admitted you. On explaining your business, she agreed to allow you to confront her husband, even though he had not long retired for the night.'

I could see where this was leading and made to protest before he went any further, but Holmes placed a firm grasp on my wrist. 'Let the inspector finish his tale,' he said, calmly.

'You already knew from Mrs Clark's letters that there would be a gun to hand,' Mackie continued. 'A conversation ensued, perhaps there was an altercation, and the result was that you shot and killed Mr Clark, then quickly left the house. I must assume that any boot prints that revealed your presence in the house were cleaned away either by Mrs Clark or Mrs Pettigrew. Either you or one of the ladies positioned the gun so it would appear that Clark had shot himself. That did not, of course, fool the police. Even if it was by then too late to catch a train back to London, you could still make your way home that same night. If you set out to walk along the high street, I am sure you would have been able to beg a ride on one of the farm carts that go back and forth and be home well in time to make the train journey next morning.'

I hardly knew what to say. Taking my lead from Holmes, I remained silent.

'A nice story, pure supposition with not a shred of proof,' said my friend. 'You will not be able to find one person who will state that Stamford was in Coldwell at the time of the murder of Mr Clark, because he was not there.'

'You do not know that, Mr Holmes.'

'I know Stamford. He is telling the truth.'

Mackie looked at me. 'What do you say, Mr Stamford?'

'I have told you the truth from the start,' I said.

'Would you be prepared to be confronted by the stationmaster to see if he can determine if the man who arrived at Coldwell station on the evening of the murder was you?'

I hesitated. 'This is a dangerous proceeding,' said Holmes. 'The observation must have taken place in poor light, and men make mistakes and often say what they think the enquirer wishes to hear. I doubt very much that he would be capable of being positive about the identity of the man unless it was someone he knew well.'

'I accept what you say,' said Mackie. 'If I agree to take that into account, would you agree to the test?' He looked at me searchingly. There was no indication from Holmes that I should not.

'On that understanding, yes,' I said.

'Did you know about the death of Mrs Clark's former employer, Mr Jeffs?'

Here I was on firmer ground. 'Lily told me that Mrs Clark, Miss Kenrick as she was then, had been a housekeeper until her employer died. The other details I only discovered at the inquest. I know it looks bad for Mrs Clark, but the more I see her, the better I know her. I have been impressed by her truthfulness, her intelligence, her courage. I think that if she ever committed any wrongdoing, she would admit to it and take the consequences.'

Mackie nodded thoughtfully. 'I will arrange for a meeting with the stationmaster now, if possible, then I will have a word with your cousin, after which I will return to Romford and interview Mrs Clark. My advice to you, Mr Stamford, is to remain in Coldwell for the time being. You are not under arrest, but I regard you as someone of interest in this case.'

'I have nothing to hide,' I said.

'As to Mrs Clark, I agree that she is a lady of courage and intelligence. She may also be extremely dangerous, but that is to be determined.'

'Inspector, might I ask you something?' said Holmes.

'Of course.'

'The delivery boy, Harry Gibson. What has been done to locate him? Unlike Stamford, he was at or near the house on the night of the murder.'

Mackie gave a rueful smile. 'We have traced his sweetheart and she has confirmed that she expected him to visit. In fact, it was his intention that day to make his delivery round at least an hour earlier than usual, after which he planned to walk up to Romford to see her. But he did not come, and she has heard nothing from him. The circumstances are suspicious to say the least.'

'Did anyone see him after he made his delivery at Spring Cottage?'

'There is a witness who saw him pushing the cart back to Upper Coldwell Farm. That is all.'

'And the gun and the slippers. Have they provided any clues?'

'I am afraid not. The gun is what is often referred to as a lady's pocket pistol. No known origin. Foreign manufacture. It has never previously been involved in a crime, neither does it appear on lists of stolen goods. The slippers, well, they are of good quality, very little worn. No initials or monograms.'

'Might I be permitted to examine them?'

'You are very persistent, Mr Holmes, but no. They are exhibits in a murder case. Once we have the criminal convicted, then I might oblige your curiosity, but not until then.' Mackie rose from his seat. 'But now let us see the stationmaster.'

We walked up to the railway station, with my nerves in a very unhappy state. I was extremely grateful to have Holmes by my side and believed that only his calm guidance had steadied me and saved me from arrest.

The stationmaster was going about his usual business, and was not especially pleased to see us, but was gruffly polite. 'Mr George,' said Mackie. 'We know that this gentleman, Mr Stamford, came here by train three mornings ago. You have already told me of a man who arrived here late one evening which would have been only a few hours before Mr Clark was murdered. You were unable to identify the man, and I do not expect you to do so now, but can you tell me if he bore any resemblance to Mr Stamford? Is there any possibility that it was he?'

The stationmaster looked me up and down, and chuckled. 'Naw, this gentleman is very short — I mean, my wife is taller than him. I would say the man who came up that evening was more my height.'

It is not very pleasant for a man to be reminded of his want of stature, and I almost protested at the expression 'very short', which I thought rather extreme, but decided to remain silent. I could only assume that the stationmaster's wife was tall for a female.

Mackie thanked him and we departed. 'I am prepared to agree that you were not the man who came by train that night,' he said. 'I shall make further enquiries to discover whom he might have been. But that, of course, does not prove you were not in Coldwell that night. It only proves you did not come by train.'

I didn't say it, of course, but my feeling was that if Mrs Clark had wanted to dispatch her husband, she would not have felt the need to ask a man to do it for her.

'Inspector,' said Holmes, 'may I have your assurance that the police and their appointed experts have now completed their examination of Spring Cottage?'

Mackie hesitated, then gave a curt nod. 'I know what you are about, Mr Holmes,' he said. 'Yes, do as you please. If you were to find anything which we have not, I trust you will not keep it to yourself.'

'You have my assurance on that point,' said Holmes.

Mackie went to Spring Cottage to speak to Lily, and I thanked Holmes profusely for his support. He brushed my thanks aside as if his actions were nothing. They might have been nothing to him, but they were very much something to me.

I was a little worried about Lily being interviewed by Inspector Mackie and mentioned this to Holmes. 'You may have noticed that my cousin, who is a dear girl, is very susceptible in the presence of single gentlemen, and can be apt to behave foolishly,' I said.

'Really?' said Holmes. 'I had not observed.'

'I would guess that Inspector Mackie is married, although he does not wear a ring,' I said.

'He has a wedding ring on his watch chain, and two silver tokens,' said Holmes. 'He is a widower with two children.'

This did not reassure me.

'And now,' said Holmes, 'let us return to the Plough, where I hope Mr Forbright will have remained and will be willing to tell us what he knows of the history of Mr John Clark.'

CHAPTER TWENTY-ONE

We found Mr Forbright happily settled at the Plough, enjoying a pint of beer while demolishing a hot beef pudding with noticeable enthusiasm. He was wiping the last of the gravy from his plate with a piece of bread the size of his fist when Holmes went to speak to him.

'Mr Forbright, allow me to introduce myself. My name is Sherlock Holmes, I study chemistry and anatomy at Barts Medical College, and I assisted Dr Wright in his examination of the body of Mr Clark.'

'Did you now?' exclaimed Mr Forbright. 'I hope you don't want me to talk about the inquest verdict, because that was what we all thought and there isn't much more I can say.'

'Oh, I would not presume to do so,' said Holmes. 'I see your glass is nearly empty. Might I provide you with another?'

Mr Forbright had no objection to this, and I was dispatched to the bar counter to obtain refreshments, while Holmes took a seat with the ironmonger.

There was a short pause as the last of the bread was consumed, helped on its way with copious draughts of Essex ale. 'I wished to ask you about your identification of Mr Clark,' said Holmes, when Forbright finally sat back from the table. 'Given the general lack of information about him in Coldwell, I found this very interesting. I did sense that your certainty was far more than the recall of a small scar and a broken tooth.'

Forbright chuckled and used a large napkin to wipe beer froth from his whiskers. 'Did you now? Well, you would be quite right, because I broke that tooth for him and split his lip with the same blow. And I'm not ashamed of it, either.'

'Indeed? Tell me more.'

'As I said, Clark and I both worked for his father. He was also called John. I always had my suspicions about young Clark; he wasn't quite straightforward, if you know what I mean. He had ideas that he was better than other people, thought he was something of a gentleman, which he was not. No shame in that if a man is honest and works hard. When money was missing from the shop, I knew it had to be him who had taken it. But when old Clark found out, his son told him he had seen me putting my hand in the till. I couldn't prove I was innocent, and of course the father believed the son and I was told to go. But afterwards Clark and I had a private discussion on the matter. He taunted me, and as good as said that he was guilty but would never be blamed. I made my feelings on the matter very clear.' Forbright flexed his fingers meaningfully. 'He was never happy about that scar. He grew his moustache and combed it specially to hide it as best he could. After that, times were hard for me. I couldn't find the work I was suited to, so I had to go labouring, but then about a year later Clark decided he had had enough of the hardware business and left Ilford. He had plans to make his fortune — I don't know how and I don't know if he succeeded. But when he went, he took money with him which he had stolen from the shop. That was when his father realised who the real thief was. He came to me and to give the man credit, he owned that he had been wrong and said how sorry he was not to have trusted me. He took me back. I worked hard, and we built up the business and eventually went into partnership. When his health got bad and he could no longer work, I bought out his share and gave him a pension.'

'Which means that Clark had no claim on his father's business under a will?'

'No, none.'

'He didn't come to the funeral?'

'We didn't know where he was to let him know his father had died. If you told me he was in prison, I wouldn't have been surprised. But then a few weeks ago, he turns up in Coldwell, and is shot dead in his own bed. And I couldn't help wondering if there was someone he had stolen from or cheated who wanted him dead, and who finally caught up with him. But no-one round here knew him of old.'

'He claimed to be a rich man. He told his wife he had properties in Wales.'

To our surprise, Forbright laughed. 'He used to tell that to the women he courted. He hoped to marry a lady of fortune and had to give a good account of himself. Said he owned houses in Wales, Scotland, North of England. Was it the truth? I couldn't say. I doubt it. No-one ever saw one.' He shrugged. 'Who knows? All these years later it might even be true.'

'It is as I feared,' said Holmes once Mr Forbright had gone back to his business. 'Mr Clark may be the man he claims to be, but he is and has always been an empty shell.'

'And now I am sorry to say I must interview Mr Danbury once more,' said Holmes a short while later. 'I am tempted to remonstrate with him for his handiwork, but he appears to have no shame. I have other matters to discuss, however.' He was about to go up to Danbury's room but was saved the trouble by the man he sought coming downstairs into the public bar and ordering a beer, then taking it to a table in the corner. Setting the glass before him, he took a document from his pocket and began to read it.

'A worrying missive,' said Holmes. 'Not black bordered, but it is mysterious to him, as the folding of the paper shows that he has opened and read it more than once. Now he reads it again and pauses to think.'

I was wondering if it would remain a mystery, then I reflected that nothing was a mystery to Holmes for long. It was just a matter of time before he shone the light of his intelligence upon it, and all was made clear. Danbury must have understood a little of that, because on seeing us, he hesitated then rose, took his beer in hand, and came over to our table. 'I am sorry to trouble you, gentlemen, but I have a letter here regarding the things I discussed with you recently, and it might help me order my thoughts to have other minds addressing what I have just been told.'

'That is no trouble,' said Holmes. 'Please join us.'

Danbury took a seat at our table with some alacrity. 'As I mentioned, I have been searching for the absconded rascal Mr Frederick Quintinfield, who appears to be the author of a great many crimes. London agents have also been looking for him, in case he has returned to his old haunts. But now I find that all my efforts have been in vain.' He brandished the letter, giving it a fierce little shake. 'I have just been informed that Mr Quintinfield is deceased. As I mentioned, I had heard rumours that in his youth he showed signs of a weak and melancholy disposition, and I am now told that he expired two months ago, of a brain disease, in an asylum for the insane. He was committed there on the advice of his doctor and with the agreement of his father. I have not seen the papers, but I believe everything was in order. That committal took place when he was twenty years of age, seventeen years ago.'

'Seventeen years?' I exclaimed. 'But he is said to have been working for his father more recently than that and managing the business following his father's death until six months ago. There can't have been two of them. Or —' I had a sudden moment of inspiration — 'perhaps there could have been. Maybe there were twins, one sane and one insane.'

'Both called Frederick?' queried Danbury. I was obliged to see his point. 'And he was an only son, there is no doubt of it. The mother died when he was born.'

'But the father might have had a secret family and another son who looked just like the older one,' I said. I thought from Danbury's expression that he gave some credence to that idea. He said nothing but drew a little notebook from his pocket and wrote in it.

'It might be possible,' said Holmes, drily ignoring my theory, which I thought had some merit, 'that after Mr Frederick Quintinfield spent a period of time in the asylum, he showed signs of improvement such that his father was able to obtain his release. A fond father would have wanted to have his son at home. Such a circumstance would fit some of the facts. It would explain both the son's disappearance, and the father's reluctance to tell the truth about his absence.'

'It does fit,' said Danbury. 'And I know that in more recent years the father took great pride in the fact that his trusted assistant and partner in the business was his son, Frederick. He must have been most relieved to see him cured.'

'That is only a suggestion,' said Holmes, 'but if he was released, there will be some record of it in the asylum documents.'

'I am sure there must be,' said Danbury, 'although I have no authority to examine them.'

'You had no authority to see papers relating to the demise of Mr Jeffs,' said Holmes, rather pointedly.

'That enquiry was reported in the newspapers,' said Danbury. 'Once I found the article mentioning the housekeeper, Miss

Kenrick, the coroner did the rest. Asylum papers are under a heavy seal.'

'That is a great pity,' said Holmes, 'because we have another mystery to address, on which those records would enlighten us. When and why did Frederick Quintinfield return to the asylum?'

'It might have been when he rushed away,' I said. 'Perhaps he went there to hide from the police.'

'That would not have been a wise step,' said Holmes. 'He could not have remained there undetected for long. He was there under his own name, and the newspapers were reporting his disappearance. The director would have advised the police that the fugitive they sought was within the asylum walls, and he could easily have secured the wanted man until they arrived.'

'I agree,' said Danbury. 'But now I think about it, I have another theory that might do. It has always been suspected that when Quintinfield left his business he found a safe refuge with one of his criminal associates, perhaps the same man who sent him the note which alarmed him so much that he left both his home and his business immediately. But as we now know, he was very ill, a dying man. He had a disease of the brain. He might not have known it himself, then. But when the signs of his illness became plain, this associate, unable to look after his friend, took him to the asylum. He must have been admitted under a false name, but perhaps the patient, in a moment of delirium, revealed his true identity. Even if the asylum knew he was a wanted criminal, he was also a man needing care. He must have died soon afterwards.'

Holmes and I were obliged to agree that this was possible. It was a conclusion which gave Danbury no pleasure. 'Well, it appears that my business here is over. I have a few matters to settle and once I am satisfied that there is nothing more I can do in the Quintinfield affair, I shall undertake another assignment.'

'As you have been making enquiries about the village, have you learned anything about Harry Gibson, the missing witness?' asked Holmes.

'There isn't much to say. Nineteen years of age, born in the village, late father was a labourer. Well-liked and reliable. Not known for dishonesty. Doesn't usually go wandering off without saying where he is going, but of course, the prospect of seeing a sweetheart might cloud a young man's memory.' He shrugged. 'That's all I can tell you. I expect he'll turn up.'

'You have not been engaged to discover the murderer of Mr Clark?' I asked.

'Oh, I always suspected the wife,' said Danbury with a chuckle. 'It usually is the wife. Young woman, rich older man. Killed for his fortune. I expect there is a lover somewhere. It's an old story.'

When Danbury had left us, I said, 'I think Mr Danbury's profession has given him an outlook which I cannot imagine could apply to the lady I know.'

'It may be the theme being pursued by the police,' said Holmes. 'They are hoping to discover Mrs Clark's secret paramour, a man she admitted to the house.'

'I can't believe there is any such person,' I said.

'I sincerely hope there is not.'

'Mr Pollaky's agents have been very active,' I said. 'I wonder if the police have been informed of Mr Quintinfield's death? Or perhaps they already know.'

'I am sure they do,' said Holmes.

'There is no criminal for them to arrest now.'

'No, but there might be hidden proceeds of his dealings, personal property which he has concealed somewhere, and which the rightful owners would wish to have returned to them. I don't have the resources or the authority of a police force, but I know one London policeman who would take notice of my conclusions and pursue the matter. I will write to Sergeant Lestrade.'

CHAPTER TWENTY-TWO

When we returned to Spring Cottage, Lily's ordeal under the fire of Inspector Mackie's questioning was over. I need not have worried about her setting her cap at the inspector, as she was clearly very annoyed with him. 'I did not like that policeman,' she said. 'He asked me all kinds of questions and some of them were quite insolent. I am only glad that Mrs Pettigrew was allowed to sit with me, as it would have been quite horrid otherwise.'

'What was the theme of his enquiries?' asked Holmes.

'Oh, he wanted to know all of poor Una's history. I think he was looking for something in her character or her past which would mark her out as a murderess. As we all know, there was nothing, and I told him so. I said he ought to be ashamed of himself for arresting an innocent lady. That old gentleman she kept house for, he was almost ninety, and always walking about the house even though his legs were bad, and sometimes he forgot his stick and she had to help him. I was not at all surprised when I heard he had taken a fall.'

'I presume the inspector has now gone to Romford to interview Mrs Clark.'

'Yes. But he will find she will not crumble and admit to anything she has not done. I know her too well to fear that. Do you think he will charge her with murder?'

'He has no direct proof,' said Holmes. 'She was in the house when the crime was committed, as was Mrs Pettigrew, but I do not, as he seems to have done, rule out the theory that an accomplished burglar might have succeeded in entering and leaving, despite the fact that there are no obvious signs that he was here.'

'You think that is possible?'

'It is not impossible; therefore I will not rule it out. And now, I will make the detailed examination of the house which I was hoping to do before the police presence prevented it. I only hope they have left me something of interest.'

Once Holmes had a magnifying glass in his hand, he was the most intense, relentless creature imaginable. I could do nothing to assist him, only watch and admire and perhaps learn. Nothing, other than a detail too small for anything other than a microscope to detect, would escape his notice. Every room, every door, every window in the house came under his scrutiny. He was already satisfied that no intruder could have come through the back bedroom window, and he was now able to establish that neither had there been any access through the other windows. There was an attic space not capable of being called a room, but nevertheless Holmes examined this, too, and announced that even if it was possible to enter via the roof, no-one had done so.

Once the interior survey was complete, he went outside, looking at the wall, the drainage, the ivy, the paths, and the earth. After examining the lock and bolt of the front door, he announced that he entirely agreed with the evidence of the locksmith, then he proceeded to the back door. The crack in the mortar was easily visible; in fact I wondered if it was my imagination, but it seemed that it was a little wider than when I had seen it last. Holmes struck a match and peered inside, then he examined the steps that led up to the door. He said nothing at this point, but moved on to a survey of the garden, and the contents of the dilapidated shed which could be reached by the path of flat stones sunk into the soil. Part of the ruined building was unusable, but one corner was still protected from the elements, and kept tolerably clean and tidy. There was a small shelf on which rested some gardening tools of a size suitable for the hands of a lady, and some blank metal markers.

Once his searches were complete, Holmes decided to retire indoors to ruminate on his findings. Mrs Pettigrew was busy about the house and Lily, still unhappy at the cruelty of Inspector Mackie, was soothing herself with a little book she had found on the kitchen shelf, called *The Secret Lore of Flowers*. Since Mrs Pettigrew did not favour smoking in the house, we decided to take luncheon at the Plough where no-one would object or even notice if Holmes filled his pipe with his customary strong tobacco. Once the pipe was half smoked, he expounded on his thoughts.

'The locksmith,' he said, 'told the court that no illegal entry had been made by the front door, and in that I concur. As regards the back door, he believed a skilled man might have been able to slide the bolt and return it. There are some slight scratches in the mortar which suggest that this might have happened, but it is also possible that these were made when the bolts were installed. I must also consider the builder Mr Clark was advised to consult, Mr Oakes. I have written to him asking him to come and discuss what advice he gave if such a meeting took place. He might have inspected the crack and made those marks. I can detect a slight scrape from a metal tool, but there is also some wear which could have been from the sliding of a cord, which is more suggestive of a burglar.'

'That would be a hard thing to achieve in the dark,' I said. 'If Dr Wright is correct, when Mr Clark was killed it was full dark apart from moonlight. And why did this intruder leave no footprints?'

'He did leave footprints of a sort,' said Holmes. 'You recall I observed some light smudges? The boots wrapped in sacking were not those of the delivery boy, who, we have been told, did not employ them, but our intruder. If I had been permitted to follow them, I would know a great deal more than I do now. But I did find something.'

Holmes made one of his infuriating pauses as he tamped down the tobacco in his pipe, added a fresh charge, drew on it strongly, and made sure to have it burning well before he continued. He did this deliberately, so there was no point in my urging him on.

'If there was an intruder, he was taking great care to leave no sign that he had been there. But to work the lock and the bolt, and operate the cord, he needed light. He was working in near dark, although there was the light of the moon, sufficient for simple purposes, but not this. Situated with the house between himself and the road, he was hidden from view. Behind him were only fields. He might have carried a small lantern, or, more common still, a stub of candle and some matches. I was looking to see if there was a drop of candle wax on the step. A half-burned match was too much to hope for, given the weather and the passage of time. Unfortunately, I found neither.'

'Oh,' I said.

'I was not altogether surprised, as I thought had they been there they would have been discovered by the police or the locksmith, both of whom are familiar with the ways of burglars, and we would have learned of it at the inquest. But I decided to take a wider look, near to the little garden, where I found the thread of hessian. And it was there, in the soil, that I found the candle wax, not a mere drop, but a splash, as if the candle had been shaken or dropped on the ground. I cannot imagine that Mrs Pettigrew tends the garden at night by candlelight; therefore, someone has been there in the darkness, and recently.'

'The delivery boy? Would he have used a candle?'

'Not impossible, but after carrying out that work for a number of years he knew his way about. All he had to do was leave his delivery on the step, and the light of the moon was quite sufficient for that.'

'But what about the lock? Had it been picked? The locksmith said not.'

'I agree. It was not. But consider this. If an intruder without means of entry had been let in deliberately by an occupant of the house, that person would surely have undone both bolt and lock to admit him. Could the door have been left bolted but unlocked? That is possible, although unlikely. Might Mrs Pettigrew have been careless? Again, possible but unlikely. Our final theory is that our intruder had a key. How he might have come in possession of one, I do not know.'

'But you do believe there was an intruder?' I exclaimed.

'It is a strong possibility. But unfortunately, we cannot prove when those marks in the mortar were made unless someone admits they made them. And if Mrs Clark was tried for murder, the prosecution would dismiss the slight scratches and the trace of candle wax as ambiguous, and they would carry far less weight than the more obvious case against the wife. I still have a long way to go.'

CHAPTER TWENTY-THREE

Holmes had promised Inspector Mackie to advise the police of anything he might discover and was as good as his word. Since the inspector was in Romford, he went to Rose Cottage to pass the news of finding the spilt wax to Constable Higgs, who said he would notify his superior. 'The result was as anticipated,' said Holmes on his return. 'Any unusual findings are being attributed to the delivery boy, who has still not been found. I did learn that enquiries are being made in case the watch has recently been offered for sale, which have also proved unsuccessful. If nothing else, I hope I might plant a seed of doubt in the inspector's mind. He is not a foolish man, but somewhat inflexible.'

We returned to Spring Cottage hoping to hear news of Mrs Clark, but there was none. Mrs Pettigrew provided tea and fruit cake, but we were unable to give her undoubted skill the attention it deserved. There is something about waiting for news in a state of uncertainty which does not assist the appetite. Lily was persuaded to join us, but it was a gathering in which all we could do was discuss again and again what facts we knew and did not know, and the conversation yielded nothing.

We were abruptly disturbed by the ringing of the doorbell followed almost immediately by a loud thumping on the front door.

'Someone is very impatient to be let in,' I said. 'It cannot be Mrs Clark, as she has a key.'

'I hope it isn't that horrid Mr Rowe,' said Lily. 'Una told me all about him. He has come to steal things, I am sure of it.'

'Stay where you are,' said Holmes. 'We will go to the door.'

On our way we encountered Mrs Pettigrew in the hallway, looking very worried. 'No-one ever knocks like that,' she said. The bell sounded again, and the knocking became even louder and more insistent. The housekeeper was more than content to let the gentlemen deal with the unexpected arrival.

Holmes strode to the front door and threw it open. The man who stood on the doorstep was a portly individual of about fifty with a ruddy face. He was attired in coarse working clothes and a battered hat, but from his manner it was obvious that his work mainly consisted of giving the orders while the two younger men who accompanied him did the heavy labour. One was so like the older man in face and body that I guessed he was a son; the other was taller, thinner, and paler, with a close-fitting cap on his head.

'Oh,' said the man on the step, surprised at seeing Holmes. 'And who might you be?'

'I might ask the same,' said my friend, evenly. 'My name is Sherlock Holmes, of Barts Medical College. I recently assisted Dr Wright at the post-mortem examination of Mr Clark. This is my associate, Mr Stamford. If you have called to see Mrs Clark, she is not at home.'

'Well, I was expecting Mrs Clark, but my business can be done without her present,' said the man, undaunted. He took a creased and grubby card from his pocket and handed it to Holmes. 'Robert Cutter and Son of Ilford; we buy and sell furniture and all household effects. I have come to collect my property.' With a jerk of the thumb, he indicted a heavy wagon standing outside the cottage, to which two large but patient horses were harnessed.

'Your property?' exclaimed Holmes. 'I am aware that you offered to buy the contents of the cottage from Mrs Clark before she was married, but she told me she had refused to sell. Nothing here can be your property.'

'It is and I have the papers to prove it,' said Cutter, in an assured and business-like manner, pulling some papers from inside his coat. 'I have bought all the furniture, chinaware, iron and copper plate, silverware, linens, brushes; it is all listed here. I expect we'll need several visits to clear it all.'

'Let me see,' said Holmes with a frown.

Cutter handed him the papers. 'Bill of sale,' he said. 'All legal.'

The bill ran to several pages, all on headed paper and tied together at one corner with a length of tarry string. It consisted of a written list of the contents of the cottage by category. Holmes made a careful study, page by page, the last one ending with the signatures of Robert Cutter and John Clark, a price, and a date. It had been signed two days before Clark was murdered.

Mrs Pettigrew came forward and Mr Cutter saluted her with a broad grin. Her expression was not so friendly. 'Mrs Clark would never have sold her things to you or anyone!' she said. Then she gasped. 'Clem!'

The thinner of the two younger men smiled ruefully. 'Aunt Ada,' he said. 'You're looking well.'

'That's more than I can say of you,' she said sternly. 'What are you doing here?'

He shrugged. 'Well, as you see, I am now apprenticed to a trade.'

'I thought you were in London.'

'I was, where Her Majesty the Queen provided me with some very close accommodation, all found. Eight months. But she was kind enough to allow me out. I have been a free man since yesterday morning. I thought my old master Mr Cutter might find honest work to keep me on the straight and narrow, and here I am.'

Mrs Pettigrew looked extremely dubious about the prospect of Mr Cutter offering someone anything resembling honest work.

Holmes had completed his reading of the document. 'Mrs Pettigrew, please bring me the marriage certificate of Mr and Mrs Clark.' After a moment of surprise, she realised the import of the question and hurried away.

'If you want to satisfy yourself as to the signature, feel free,' said Cutter. 'Mr Clark came to see me last week, and we made the deal. Thirty guineas. All properly signed, and to be paid for on collection. I have the money here.' He patted his pocket.

'Mrs Clark has made no mention of this.'

'Hasn't she now? Well, no matter, the property was Mr Clark's to do with as he pleased. What he chose to tell his wife is his business.'

'Did he make any mention of his wife? Of his plans for the property?'

'No, and I didn't ask him.'

Mrs Pettigrew returned with the certificate, and Holmes made a comparison of the signature of the groom and the one on the sale document.

'Are they the same?' I asked.

'At a cursory glance, yes, and as far as I am aware this certificate is the only example of Mr Clark's signature to hand.' He returned the bill to Mr Cutter.

'So,' said Cutter, tucking away the papers in his coat and rubbing his hands together in anticipation, 'we may proceed?'

'You may not,' said Holmes. 'Even if, as this document suggests, you have an agreement to purchase the portable property in this house, you do not own Spring Cottage, which is the property of Mrs Clark. As a widow, she has the power to decide all legal matters concerning the cottage. It is therefore up to Mrs Clark as to whom she permits to enter her home, and I am quite sure that you are not amongst those persons.'

'I am entitled to remove my property,' said Cutter. 'Once I hand over the money, it is mine.'

'I imagine that had Mr Clark been here, he would have accepted the payment and allowed you to remove the property, but he is not,' said Holmes. 'I cannot imagine Mrs Clark who now owns the property would do either. I should add that there are currently enquiries afoot as to the legality of the marriage. This would affect the entitlement of Mr Clark to take possession of the effects and sell them. I suggest that you delay your business until Mrs Clark returns and the enquiries are resolved.'

Mr Cutter grunted with frustration, but Holmes's tone had been reasonable, his arguments beyond dispute. 'Very well, but I'll be back next week,' he said. 'And then we'll see what the law has to say about it.' He directed his men back to the wagon with a jerk of the head. Clem gave a grin and a wave to his aunt before he left, then sauntered away, scratching the back of his neck where a few tufts of black hair were itching his shorn scalp. Holmes watched the men climb back into the vehicle and urge the horses back in the direction of Ilford.

'I will see that Mr Philpott knows of this,' said Holmes.

Mrs Pettigrew nodded unhappily. 'I had heard a rumour that Clem was in prison for stealing,' she said, 'but I wasn't willing to believe it. I shall pray he finds better employment. I don't mind him doing rough work; I expect he had far worse to do in prison. Did you see how torn and scraped his hands are? But I'm afraid that Mr Cutter drives too close to what is illegal and can't be trusted.'

'Your nephew seemed very confident that Mr Cutter would give him work,' said Holmes.

'Yes, well, the son, Charlie, they were once drinking companions.' She was unwilling to go into further detail and returned to the kitchen.

'You see what this means, Stamford?' said Holmes.

'More trouble for Mrs Clark,' I said. 'It will be hard and quite possibly more expensive than the effects are worth to disprove that paper.'

'We have been looking for a potential intruder who committed the murder of Mr Clark,' said Holmes, 'and the Cutter family were good suspects, since we have been told they are adept in that line of work. By the by, I notice that the bill of sale does not include the watch. Clark took care to keep it for himself. But I think that when Mr Cutter came here before Mrs Clark was married, and looked about him, he saw something of more than usual value, on which he could turn a tidy profit. However, he would be most unlikely to try and steal property which he has already bought. If the document is a forgery, he remains a suspect. If it is genuine, its implications are extremely serious for Mrs Clark.'

CHAPTER TWENTY-FOUR

We were hoping that Mrs Clark would be allowed to return to her home that evening, but when Mr Philpott visited us later that day, he was alone.

'Mrs Clark has been questioned very thoroughly,' he said, 'but the inspector cannot make a case against her unless she confesses, and I am sure she will not. In fact, I am prepared to stake my reputation on her complete innocence. But she has been given a dinner and will be made as comfortable as possible for the night. He will resume his questioning in the morning. I shall return early and make a strong case for her early release without charge. The inspector has at last confirmed that the examination of the body of Mr Clark is complete, and it may be interred, and I have some important news on that front.' We waited expectantly as he removed some papers from his document case. 'Following the revelations at the inquest, I directed my clerk to make enquiries about the deceased's family, and he has informed me that as stated by Mr Forbright the late Mr Clark was indeed the son of a Mr John Clark senior, who was a hardware merchant in Ilford. There are no living siblings. Mrs Clark died when her son was only ten years old. And there is a family burial plot at the parish church of St Mary's. The police have confirmed that the funeral arrangements should proceed, and the undertakers will come tomorrow morning to remove the body.'

'Thank you, Mr Philpott,' said Holmes. 'I only wish that I too had good news to report, but I am sorry to say there was a recent visitor to Spring Cottage whom I was obliged to send on his way. In due course it will be necessary to inform Mrs Clark, who I am sure would value your advice.'

'Not that scoundrel Rowe?' said Philpott, with a frown.

'No, it was this person,' said Holmes, producing Cutter's business card.

'Oh, what a nuisance,' said Philpott, who clearly knew the man by reputation. 'Whatever did he want? Seeking to purchase the effects, I suppose. Even if Mrs Clark did decide to do so, I would not advise her to sell to Cutter, who is untrustworthy to say the least.'

'Mr Cutter showed me a document signed by Mr Clark. If it is genuine, and the signature does match that on the marriage certificate, it shows that two days before his death Clark sold all the portable effects in the cottage to Mr Cutter for thirty guineas.'

'He did what?' exclaimed Philpott. 'Mrs Clark has said nothing to me about this.'

'I rather fear that was because she knew nothing of it. Mr Cutter brought his wagon and his men and said he had come to take away his property.'

Philpott looked about him in alarm as if to discover what might be missing. 'I see you did not permit him to do so.'

'I did not allow him or his men to enter the house. Even if the movables had been his by agreement, he had no right of entry, which only Mrs Clark can allow. But he will be back, I am sure of it. All I have achieved is to delay him so our investigations can continue. The document may prove to be a forgery. If it is shown to be genuine, it will be hard to deny him. Our best hope is to discover another prior marriage for Clark, which would invalidate this one.'

Philpott sighed wearily. 'If Clark had married Miss Kenrick under a false name, he would not have been entitled to the property, but I have uncovered nothing to suggest he wasn't exactly who he claimed to be. If he did marry before, how am I to find the evidence?' He made a helpless gesture. 'There are hundreds of John Clarks. Perhaps a legal wife will come forward and claim him, or someone who knew him in the past will recall a wedding. But I shall make further efforts. And I will call on Mr Cutter tomorrow and see the paper for myself.'

Once again Holmes and I made ourselves comfortable at the Plough, while Lily stayed at Spring Cottage. I think we had the best of the accommodation, and that was no fault of Mrs Pettigrew, who did her best with a house where no matter what one did, draughts and rain always seemed to find a way in.

When we had breakfasted, we went to see if there was any news, and found that the undertakers had already removed the corpse of Mr Clark and were hoping to hold the funeral in two days' time.

The newspapers had by now shown an interest in the case, and that morning's *Times* sported the headline 'Remarkable Case of Shooting in Essex,' reporting that a businessman had been shot dead in his bed with a pistol fired through his own slipper. People often express a particular horror at being attacked in their beds, as if that is in some way worse than being attacked anywhere else. I suppose it is the innocent helplessness of the sleeping individual in the one place they ought to feel safe and secure which makes the crime appear most terrifying.

Soon afterwards, Inspector Mackie and Constable Simmons called, bringing Mrs Clark and Mr Philpott with them. The solicitor informed us that his client would not be charged with any crime but had been told that she remained under suspicion for the time being and must not leave Coldwell. She was at once whisked away to be soothed by Lily. We expected the police to depart but they did not, and when Mrs Pettigrew made to return to the kitchen, Inspector Mackie advised her to remain where she was.

To my annoyance, the inspector, showing every sign of being wholly unrepentant for what I thought was an unreasonable pursuit of a blameless lady, had turned his attention to the worthy housekeeper. 'I would like to speak to you once more,' he said. 'That may be done here or at the station, as you wish.'

'We may speak here,' said Mrs Pettigrew. 'I have a pudding to boil and do not wish to delay the preparations.' She stared at Mackie as if she might like to boil him, too. 'Am I suspected of anything?'

'Not at present,' said Mackie, 'but I am obliged to consider that you were the only other person apart from Mrs Clark who was in the house when Mr Clark was shot.'

'As far as you know,' she said.

'I would appreciate it if I could have more information on that point,' he said. 'If there is anything you recall which you have not yet told me, now is the time to do so.'

Mackie and Simmons accompanied Mrs Pettigrew to the kitchen, while Holmes and I remained in the parlour and Mr Philpott decided to stay in case he was needed.

'I have seen Mr Cutter,' he said, 'and he was positively eager to show me the bill of sale. I examined it very carefully but could see nothing to suggest it was not perfectly genuine. As far as I have been able to discover, John Clark was the lawful owner of the personal property in this house and was fully entitled to sell it if he wished.'

'But why would he do such a thing?' I asked. 'Perhaps — and I know this is being charitable to him, but perhaps he did have some funds put away that we have not yet discovered and wanted to sell the old effects to replace them with new ones.'

'Without telling his wife or housekeeper?' said Holmes.

I was about to suggest that Clark might not have been the monster he had been made out to be and was intending to surprise his wife and housekeeper with new furnishings, china, and silverware, but that sounded like the kind of thing more likely to be encountered in a work of fiction than reality. I wondered if I ought to suggest the idea to Mr Danbury.

'There is one explanation I can think of,' said Holmes. 'Clark had told his wife that he intended to go to Wales to deal with the sale of properties and might be absent for some time. But no trace has been found of properties in Wales or anywhere else. And Mr Forbright, who identified Clark, told us that as a young man he often lied about his wealth when courting ladies with property. I rather fear that Clark's intention was to go away and not return. He sold the effects to raise money. By stating his intention to make a lengthy visit, it would have been some weeks before any search was made for him, giving him ample time to disappear. He was going to desert his wife.'

'Oh, the poor lady!' I exclaimed. 'As if she has not enough grief to contend with.'

'Suppose it to be true and she had discovered his plan, that would add some fuel to the inspector's suspicions,' said Philpott. 'A lady faced with the shame of desertion and its consequences might well have wanted to free herself of her husband. I fear we are obliged to mention Mr Cutter's claims to the police, but of course we are a long way from accepting them as genuine.'

I am not sure what Mrs Pettigrew said to Inspector Mackie, but it must have been interesting, since when he departed some half an hour later his ears were a little red and the constable was suppressing a smile. Mrs Pettigrew appeared unflustered as usual. 'Would you like coffee now?' she said. 'Mrs Clark and Miss Hargreaves will join you.'

When the ladies came to sit with us, I saw that Mrs Clark was more angered than distressed at her ordeal and had much to say about the accusatory manner of the inspector. 'I feel as if every part of my life and parentage has been turned inside out like a patched gown and examined for flaws,' she said. Her birthmark was even more apparent than usual. When she was suffused by emotion, it blazed red, and she wore it proudly like a jewel. I wondered if the late Mr Clark had seen her only as a vulnerable woman suitable for his purpose of acquiring her property, but had he lived, he would have found her stronger than he had supposed.

Given the antiquity of the cooking arrangements, Mrs Pettigrew made an excellent pot of coffee accompanied by plain cake. Once she had left us, Mr Philpott informed Mrs Clark, taking great care with his words, that Mr Cutter had come to her door asking about the household effects.

'Oh, I suppose now I am a widow I shall have vultures of all types trying to cheat me,' she said, dismissively.

'Mr Holmes was good enough to send him on his way,' said Philpott. 'I take it you have at no time agreed to sell to Mr Cutter?'

'No, and I never will.'

'Your husband did not think of doing so? He never suggested replacing the old furnishings with new?'

'It was not something we discussed in any detail. We were more concerned with carrying out the repairs to the cottage itself. I know there is some fault with the plumbing, and these things only get worse if not attended to. That had to be put right first. Selling the china and brass would never have raised enough. He did think of realising the funds I inherited from my cousin in order to carry out the most essential work.'

Philpott nodded to us. He had clearly reached the conclusion that the widow knew nothing of the bill of sale. 'Yes, your husband did enquire about the funds the last time I saw him, but the nature of the investment meant it was not possible to realise the capital sum,' he said.

Mrs Clark saw the import of his questions. 'Why do you ask about Mr Cutter? Is he claiming that John had agreed to sell him some things?'

'So he says, but he is not the most honest individual in the county. If he should reappear at your door, he must be sent away and you are to advise him to speak to me.'

Mrs Clark sighed at this new complication. We ate and drank in companionable silence, since no-one wished to broach the subject of her time in the Romford police cells until she did so. Once the coffee and cake were gone, Mr Philpott advised us that he had an appointment to keep. We thanked him for his services, and he left us, providing a little card with details of St Mary's parish church. I saw Mrs Clark gaze at it steadily with enough time to read the contents many times over.

'I fear,' I said to Holmes once the ladies had gone to their private deliberations, 'that you are correct, and Mr Clark had no intention of spending any more funds than necessary. He would have left as soon as he could realise enough money to make his exercise in villainy worth his while. He probably has that watch hidden away somewhere as part of his haul.'

'Yes, and it is notable that he attempted to gain hold of the capital value of the funds but was disappointed,' said Holmes. 'But one item which as far as we know he has not attempted to sell might be the most valuable of them all.'

'Oh?'

'The cottage and the land it stands on. I know it is in need of repair, any fool can see that, but I cannot judge what is required. A master builder might make something of it. The property is in Mrs Clark's name, but she could not have sold it without her husband's permission. Yet he never suggested to her that she should sell, or as far as she is aware arranged for a surveyor to place a value on it. All his promises to her took the form of repairing and improving the cottage. Why is that?' Holmes toyed with his pipe, but out of deference to Mrs Pettigrew declined to light it. 'There is something missing,' he said. 'Another piece of information which would make everything clear, but I do not as yet have it.' He grunted in annoyance. 'You know how I endeavour to acquire the knowledge and skills which will assist me in solving the mysteries I like to engage with? All else which men make such studies of I regard as unimportant. The movements of the planets and the stars, the musings of philosophers, cannot be allowed to command any part of my time or memory. Until now, I have neglected to study the professions of plumbers or master builders. And as a result, I find myself in a quandary which I hope Mr Oakes can resolve.'

CHAPTER TWENTY-FIVE

The next morning Holmes received a note from Mr Oakes to say that he would be in Coldwell on the following day to carry out some work, and would be able to meet with him in the afternoon regarding his recent conversation with John Clark about Spring Cottage. I could see that Holmes was anticipating this interview with some concern. 'I hope that Mr Oakes has something of value to divulge,' he said, 'some fact that would advance the possibility of an intruder, unknown to either of the ladies residing in the house, the fact that will help free Mrs Clark of suspicion. I am aware, however, that he might have nothing of value, or worse still, something that would destroy my case altogether.' Holmes did not say so, but he had seen for himself and appreciated Mrs Clark's intelligence and strength of character. I was sure that he would have had no hesitation in exposing her as a murderess if the facts proved it, but he would do so with considerable reluctance, and then do all he could to make a case for mercy.

The weather was not of the kind that encouraged country walks, and Holmes spent some time with his pipe and his thoughts.

I went to Spring Cottage, to see if there was any news, and found Lily and Mrs Clark in comforting conference. There was nothing to learn except that Mrs Pettigrew had requested and been granted a half day and had gone to Ilford.

'She has confessed all about her nephew, Clem Barnes,' said Mrs Clark, 'and has gone to see him. He is the son of her only sister, and she has always been fond of him, but despaired when he showed signs of turning to thievery. Since he is a convicted criminal, she thought I would forbid him to come to the house. I am not sure I will. If he has paid the price of his crime and repented, and means never to break the law again, then I would not continue his punishment beyond that which the court imposed.'

'He is working for Mr Cutter now, and his is thought to be a very suspect business,' I said.

'I know, but perhaps given his circumstances he could find no other employment. But I will see what she has to tell me when she returns.'

We were having tea when Mrs Pettigrew came back, looking tired and despondent, and we sat her down and poured a fresh cup for her. 'I thought he would have settled by now and be married and have a proper trade, but it is not to be,' she said.

'What age is he?' asked Lily.

'He is thirty-four. Prison has changed him. He was a handsome boy. Such lovely, dark, wavy hair. They shaved his head in prison. It marks him out as a convict, which its why he wears a cap until it grows back. But it was young Charlie Cutter who led him astray, put ideas in his head that money didn't always come from hard work. I fear that it will not be long before he turns to stealing again. I can't help but be glad he was still in prison when Mr Clark died, or he would surely have been suspected.'

'Was he always a thief?' said Lily. 'Or did he have a trade?'

'He used to work for the Cutters before he went away, and he told me that in London he did something in much the same line,' said Mrs Pettigrew. 'It can be an honest trade if the man is honest. But I am sure he did some business with the Cutters whenever he visited Coldwell. Selling the things he had stolen, I expect.'

'Perhaps,' said Lily dreamily, 'if he were to meet a young lady, and fall in love, he would change his ways.'

'Did he tell you anything about —' I interrupted Lily's fanciful line of conversation, but then hesitated, as I wasn't quite sure how much to reveal. 'Is Mr Cutter intending to come here again?'

'No, he only said that his employer is a patient and very determined man. He is like a dog that bites and refuses to let go until he has had what he wants.'

Mrs Clark understood the reason for my hesitation. 'Mrs Pettigrew has told me about the document Mr Cutter brought,' she said. 'I realise that you and Mr Holmes and Mr Philpott were being kind in not mentioning it when I was so weary having just returned from Romford, but I am able now to learn all the news, be it good or bad. Given what we know of Mr Cutter, there is a very good chance the bill of sale is a forgery. Mr Philpott will be sure to do all he can to prove it.' She smiled, and it was the first time in a while I had seen her do so. 'I can be patient, too.'

I returned to the Plough to take my luncheon, which was hearty if plain. There was some very fine cheese which was as good a cheese as I have ever eaten. If Holmes had come to any conclusions after his tobacco-inspired reverie, he was not yet prepared to share them with me. We were completing our meal when Constable Higgs arrived. I thought he was on general village business, but instead he approached our table directly.

'Mr Holmes,' he said, a little diffidently, 'I know this is a small matter, and I can hardly imagine it has any significance, but you asked to be informed if anything happened out of the common way.'

'I did,' said Holmes, 'and I would be most interested to hear what you have to report.' He waved the constable to a chair, and he sat with us.

'I mentioned the other day about Mr Willans and Mr Sharp and how they are always quarrelling. Their farms are adjacent to each other, up at the west of the village, Ilford way. On the edge of Mr Sharp's smallholding is an old boundary stone. It's a small one and marks the place between his land and that of Mr Willans. Late last night Mr Sharp was alerted by his dog, Grey, making a fuss. When he went out to look, he didn't notice anything amiss, but this morning when it was light, he saw the stone had gone. He says Mr Willans must have stolen it. I spoke to Mr Willans, who said he knew nothing about it.'

'The theft of an old boundary stone,' said Holmes. 'That does have a certain novelty.'

'I have never seen anything like it before. Why would anyone want such a thing? As I told you, the two have been on bad terms for many years. Sharp says Willans has moved it so he can lay claim to some of his land, but that doesn't make sense. Everyone knows where the boundary is.'

'Is it of a size that can be lifted by one man?'

'It is. About so much,' added Higgs, indicating with his hands something a foot square. 'Rounded top, about four inches thick, and whatever was carved on it once is half worn away. But everyone round here knows it.'

'And I assume that thorough searches have already been made.'

'Yes, it's not on Mr Willans's property.'

'Are there any cart tracks nearby to show it has been transported away?'

'Nothing from last night.'

'How far might one man carry such a thing?'

'Not all that far. Two men could take it quite some way easily. But why would they?'

'Perhaps it has simply sunk into the mud after all the rain.'

Higgs looked suddenly shamefaced. 'Yes, of course, you are right Mr Holmes, and I am sorry to have troubled you over such a small matter.'

'Not at all,' said Holmes. 'Sometimes the small matters can be the most interesting. The rain has ceased at long last, and I shall take a look.'

Holmes turned to me. 'Stamford, your shoes are quite unsuitable for such an expedition.'

I was happy to agree since I was hoping to remain cosily indoors and order another glass of the Plough's country beer.

'We shall have to see if there are any you might borrow.'

It was useless to protest. Constable Higgs said he had a spare set of boots, but his feet looked like those of a giant next to mine. At Spring Cottage, the same difficulty attended the late Mr Clark's walking shoes, and a pair that had once belonged to Mr Brampton. We discovered, however, that Mrs Pettigrew's gardening boots, which she usually wore lined with thick woollen socks, would fit me tolerably well, and thus clad, I set off down the high street with Holmes and the constable in search of a missing stone.

CHAPTER TWENTY-SIX

The recent rain had created a slippery layer over the drier mud, which made walking especially hard for me in my borrowed boots. I almost lost my balance several times. As we passed a hedgerow, Holmes took a heavy jack-knife from his pocket and cut a staff for us both.

When we reached our destination, the mystery only deepened. The smallholdings of Mr Sharp and Mr Willans clearly needed no boundary markers, as one was ploughed land bordered by hedges and ditches and the other a poultry farm.

Mr Willans was understandably a man who did not encourage uninvited visitors. Over a securely fastened gate, we saw a line of large poultry houses constructed from wooden boards, and smaller sheds of the type used as grain stores. Beside these were well laid out runs for the fowls, surrounded by high wirework fences. The fowls were busy pecking at the grass, looking for what nourishment might have incautiously emerged to the surface following the recent rain. All looked to be very tidy and well maintained.

Mr Willans, an active-looking individual with a leather bag of tools at his waist, was out inspecting his fences and when he saw us approach, he came to the gate to speak to us. 'I hope Mr Sharp has not been up to his tricks again,' he said. 'I want nothing to do with that man. Why he thinks I would tramp about on his land and take that stone, I can't imagine. I have better things to do. I think he has trained his dog to bark at me whenever it sees me.'

'I thought we would have another look for the stone,' said Higgs, 'and I have brought some assistance. We think it might have sunk into the mud, what with the recent rain.'

'Like as not,' said Willans. 'I hope you find it so I can be left in peace.' He turned and went back to his work.

We continued on our way to Mr Sharp's land. A gate led to a farmyard, where there was a drab cottage and a clutter of carts and muddy farm equipment. We were greeted by the sound of a barking dog, and the owner, a tall, broad-shouldered man of about forty with unkempt hair and whiskers, emerged from the cottage with the animal on a leash and approached us. 'Take care with Grey; he does not like strangers,' said Higgs. 'Or Mr Willans. I am not sure if he likes me, either.'

The dog, a large mastiff the colour of whose coat had inspired his name, was straining to get at us, and I hoped Mr Sharp had good control of it.

Sharp turned and called out, 'Martha!' and a slender woman of about his age came out of the cottage wiping her hands on her apron, and took charge of the dog, which suddenly became as docile and friendly as a puppy. She petted it and took it indoors.

'What can I do for you, Higgs?' demanded the farmer.

'We have come to take another look for the missing stone,' said Higgs. 'I don't think it can have gone far.'

'No, well, it's about as far as Willans took it,' said Sharp.

'Before I make any accusations, I want to be sure everywhere has been searched,' said Higgs.

Sharp shrugged. 'If you must. I'll be sowing the main field soon, so make it quick.'

'Might I ask what time your excellent dog barked last night?' asked Holmes.

'It would have been about two or three in the morning,' said Sharp.

'And you saw nothing?'

'No, Willans must have been here and run off when he heard the dog.'

'The constable has already told me that your dog made no fuss on the night Mr Clark was killed.'

'That's right. When he scents trouble, he lets it roar. He's a good 'un.'

'Kindly show me where the stone was situated,' said Holmes.

Sharp led the way. Close by the roadside there was a shallow rectangular hole, filled with dirty rainwater. Holmes and Higgs examined it carefully. 'Lifted it clean out,' said Sharp. 'You're not going to tell me it was loosened by the rain and slipped over.'

'No, I agree, it was well bedded in,' said Holmes, 'although the recent wet weather did play a part, softening the ground and making it easier to remove. There are signs that whoever took it had to work it back and forth before he could lift it. This was no accident.' He stood up and looked carefully about him. 'We don't know that the thief simply took it away from your land. Why would he do so? How did he do so? It has no value. Surely, Mr Sharp, even if it was planted elsewhere, it would not fool anyone into thinking that the boundary had changed.'

Sharp grunted. 'He'd like it to. Maybe he took it just to annoy me.'

'In that case, it may not have gone far. I am confident that he did not bury it in the ploughed field,' said Holmes. 'There is no disturbance of the ploughing, no footmarks, neither do I see anywhere the marks left by the wheels of a handcart that might have been used to transport it. I do see some signs of boot prints at the side of the field, the unploughed part, but the recent rain has rendered them indistinct. Now, if I was going to conceal such an item simply in the spirit of amusing myself at the expense of another, what better place than a mud-filled ditch? It is nearby, all concealing; the stone would sink to the bottom, and likely be hard to recover. Let us follow the line of the ditch.'

We proceeded along the edge of the ploughed soil, but after a few steps Holmes stopped very suddenly. 'Yes, see here, something very interesting indeed.' He bent down and studied what appeared to be a tiny wisp of something sunken into the earth. 'Do you see?'

'It's just a bit of old sacking,' said Higgs.

'That proves it,' said Sharp, triumphantly. 'Willans stores his poultry feed in sacks. He was here.'

'Gentlemen,' said Holmes, 'I ask you to look at this thread very carefully and observe the depth it has sunk into the mud. Constable, make a note.' Higgs gave me a look as if to question what Holmes was about.

I merely shrugged. 'I am sure he has a very good reason,' I said.

Higgs accepted the position and after examining the thread without disturbing it, wrote in his notebook. Holmes then took out his jack-knife, extended the blade, and lifted his find, which he placed in one of the envelopes he always seemed to have in his pocket. 'When I return to Barts, a microscope might enlighten me further,' he said. 'If it can be compared with other examples commonly used in this village, it might be possible to identify its origins. I promise nothing, however.'

As Holmes walked on beside the ditch, he used his staff to probe the murky waters. He encountered little resistance, the usual mire of mud and leaves, but after a few minutes we heard a noise as the staff struck something hard. He stopped and tapped again. 'Yes,' he said, 'we may have something here. Let us see what we may find. It is not very far below the surface.' Holmes used the staff to judge the size and shape of the submerged item.

Sharp confirmed that it matched the dimensions of the boundary stone. 'The tricky villain!' he exclaimed. 'But he was no match for you!'

I was concerned that we would not be able to lift the stone from its watery grave without breaking our backs, but Sharp was determined to take it out there and then.

'If we brace ourselves, gentlemen,' said Holmes, 'we may be able to get sufficient purchase on the drier earth, and I am sure that what one man is able to carry four of us may lift.'

It was not a wide ditch, and Holmes, with his long legs, was able to stand astride it. Higgs did likewise, while Sharp and I, taking a stand at the side of the ditch furthest from the hedgerow, stood prepared to receive the stone once it was risen. Sharp, in his heavy farmer's boots, looked steady enough, but my borrowed poorly fitting ones were not an advantage.

It was a tricky, slippery business, but Holmes and Higgs succeeded in getting a handhold on the sunken object, the surface of which was fortunately roughened and chipped with age. A determined effort brought it up into the air, where Sharp and I took hold and deposited it on the earth beside the ditch. There was no doubt that this was the missing stone. Our efforts inevitably disturbed the muddy water, which surged like a horrid slurry of decomposing rubbish, while bubbles of gas rose to the surface and enveloped us in a nauseating stench.

My long-legged and stoutly booted companions were able to spring to the side of the ditch to examine our find. I was not so fortunate. I had had to lay my staff to one side so I could use both hands to help with the stone, and as I stood up, my feet suddenly slipped and slithered in the mud. I struggled in vain to find a point where there was anything firm to stand on, and my panicky floundering made my position still worse, with the result that I began to slide down the side of the ditch. In desperation I attempted to place one foot on the other side to brace myself, hoping to be able to grasp a part of the hedge. Instead, I plunged face-first into the revolting sludge. I managed to avoid getting it in my mouth, but it found its way into my eyes and nose and ears and hair. It was cold and slimy, and I dreaded to think what noxious substances and horrid diseases it might contain. I tried to get my feet onto the bottom of the ditch so I could at least stand up to be helped out, but there was something lying there preventing me. I was expecting to find the rotting remains of an animal, but what met my hand as I attempted to push myself upright was not an animal. It was something I had encountered before in anatomy class. My hand was grasping the shoulder of a human corpse. I thrashed about in an effort not to stand on the body, and in doing so my other hand closed around something else, half submerged, a round, hard, smooth object like a stone or a projectile. Then, to my relief, I was seized under the armpits and Holmes and Higgs hauled me bodily from the ditch. I sat on the earth and spluttered and coughed, to avoid swallowing the filthy water. Everything I wore was saturated and stank horribly.

Holmes produced a clean handkerchief to wipe my face, and at last I was able to gasp, 'There is a body down there! And this!' When I was eventually able to open my eyes, I gazed at the object clutched in my hand. It was a gentleman's silver watch.

CHAPTER TWENTY-SEVEN

Holmes took the watch from my trembling fingers.

'Are you sure there's a body, sir?' asked Higgs. 'A human body? It might just be a log — or an animal.'

'My friend is studying medicine at Barts and should be able to make the distinction,' said Holmes.

'It was wearing clothes!' I exclaimed.

'Oh, well in that case, we'd better not disturb it any more and I'll go and tell Inspector Mackie,' said Higgs. 'He'll see about getting it lifted out. I — er — I'd better take that, sir.' Holmes, having examined the watch, was obliged with reluctance to hand it to the constable as potential evidence in a case of suspicious death.

'Is it Clark's?' I asked as Higgs hurried away.

'It fits the description we have.'

Mr Sharp rolled up his sleeves, eager to lug the boundary stone back to its accustomed place, but Holmes pointed out that as it had apparently been used to weigh down a corpse, it was evidence in a police enquiry and should be left where it was. Sharp grudgingly agreed.

'And now what shall we do with you, poor fellow?' said Holmes. I was in a sorry state, though as far as I could detect, uninjured. 'Let us see if we can get you a bath and clean clothes. I don't think you want to be seen by the drinking men at the Plough or you would never hear the end of it. We will go to Spring Cottage and deliver you to the mercy of Mrs Pettigrew.'

I did not relish the idea of passing along the high street as I was, like a walking scarecrow, or a man who had been condemned to be tarred and feathered for some unspeakable offence and was awaiting the arrival of the feathers, but Holmes suggested an alternative. Mr Sharp, who was enjoying some amusement at my appearance, was directed to fetch something that might cover me. I was stripped of my sodden outer garments, and Mr Sharp brought one of his rough coats, which was in little better condition than the mud-saturated clothes I had removed. Holmes and I trudged back to Spring Cottage. On the way my unusual attire did excite some comment, which I did my best to ignore.

When Mrs Pettigrew saw me appear at the kitchen door, she gasped, and then took charge in a brisk, motherly fashion. Ordered to the back kitchen, I was provided with hot water, soap, sponge, towels and a laundry tub. The least said of that arrangement, the better. I already had clean linen and shirts in my travelling bag, and when I emerged freshly scrubbed and dried, these had been brought and laid out together with a suit of clothes which I guessed must once have belonged to Mr Brampton. It was of old-fashioned formal cut as befitted a headmaster, but at least it was not too monstrously large for me. My muddy garments were next in the tub, but I feared they would never be the same again.

I had to apologise to Mrs Pettigrew about the gardening boots, but she said that they had seen enough mud in their time and a little more wouldn't hurt. By now she had made some hot coffee for us all and produced a little bottle of brandy from the medicine cabinet, which added a welcome touch to my cup.

I was regaling the ladies with my adventure when Constable Higgs arrived. 'The body has been taken to Mr Sharp's barn, together with the stone, and Dr Wright has been sent for. I wouldn't like to say for sure, but I think, from the clothes, it's

Harry Gibson. Farmer Overton at Upper Coldwell is coming to see it. And I've been asked to show this to Mrs Clark.' He took a cloth from his pocket and unwrapped it, revealing the silver watch now cleaned of mud and debris. 'Is this your late husband's watch?' he asked.

Mrs Clark examined it. 'Yes, I am quite sure,' she said. 'It is a very old piece, and I recall there was a slight dent in the casing. It is the same one.'

'Do you have any suggestion as to how it might have come into the ditch on Mr Sharp's farm?'

'None at all.'

'Inspector Mackie thinks that whoever the dead man might be, he might have been the man who entered this cottage, stole the watch and shot Mr Clark.' He looked hopefully at the two ladies for any comment.

'Since Mrs Pettigrew and I were asleep in our beds when my husband was killed, we are unable to enlighten you,' said Mrs Clark.

'Did Harry Gibson ever come in the house?'

'No,' said Mrs Pettigrew, 'he left his deliveries at the kitchen door.'

'I'll tell the inspector,' said Higgs.

'I believe that Dr Wright might find it useful to speak to us regarding our finding of the body,' said Holmes, 'and we are happy to assist him in his examination, should he require our services again.'

'I'll be sure to mention it.' Higgs seemed about to say something else but changed his mind and took his leave.

'I wonder what that was about?' I said.

'I expect he has been told by Inspector Mackie that we are not to play at being detectives,' said Holmes. 'I am only glad that I have an alibi for the time of Mr Clark's death, or he would be questioning me in the same way he questioned you. And now we have compounded our intrusion by discovering another body.'

'But we only went to Sharp's farm because Constable Higgs asked us to,' I protested. 'And it was just to look for a stone.'

'That may have been fortunate,' said Holmes, drily. 'But now consider if the body should prove to be that of Harry Gibson; then we have an interesting question to address. Coldwell lies on the old coach road between Ilford to the west and Romford to the east. Spring Cottage and Upper Coldwell Farm lie east of the railway station. We would have expected Gibson, once his final delivery was done, to travel east to the farm, where he would leave his delivery cart and then continue in that direction towards Romford to see his sweetheart. If he had suffered some mishap after leaving the cart, it was thought he would be found on the road between the farm and Romford. But the properties of Mr Willans and Mr Sharp are west of the station.'

'What does that mean?' I asked, but Holmes reserved his comment until he knew more.

The good doctor of Romford arrived in Coldwell not long afterwards and was pleased to accept our help. Mr Sharp's barn was large, damp and draughty. It could well have been a hundred years old and remained standing only out of obstinacy. By the time we arrived Dr Wright, who had engaged the services of a burly assistant, had the corpse stripped and washed, and laid out on a board supported by trestles. Mr Sharp, not especially pleased at this unexpected use of his barn, had been even less pleased when he was asked to supply as many candles as he possessed to illuminate the otherwise gloomy interior.

Before commencing his examination, Dr Wright questioned us closely about the discovery of the body. Constable Higgs had been right; the remains had been identified by Farmer Overton as that of his delivery boy Harry Gibson. When lifted from its muddy tomb, the corpse had been lying full length along the line of the ditch, face down.

I had only once in my studies up to that time examined the corpse of a drowned person, a woman taken from the River Thames, unknown, unclaimed. I had some familiarity with the signs of death by drowning, froth at the mouth, heavy lungs, fluid in the airways, murky water and debris in the stomach. Of course, as my instructors made clear to me, a body found in water need not have drowned. There are other possible causes of death which must be considered, such as violence, or the sudden shock of plunging into cold water which can cause the heart to stop.

'Was anything found in the pockets?' asked Holmes.

'A purse with a few coins, and a handkerchief,' said Dr Wright. 'I think once the handkerchief is washed, it will prove to be for a lady. A gift, perhaps.'

'Nothing else? Matches? A candle?'

'No, that was all.'

Our first task was an external examination. Harry Gibson might once have been a good-looking youth, but death and dirty water had taken their toll. Immersion had wrinkled and loosened the skin, a development which greatly hindered our search for possible injuries. There were no obvious puncture wounds, and we were satisfied that he had not been shot or stabbed.

Holmes had been bent over the corpse, examining the pallid skin with his magnifying glass. It was an unpleasant task. Decomposition advances more slowly in cold water, but renewed contact with air soon accelerates its progress, and its odour hung thickly in the air. After some minutes he straightened up. 'I think we might have a cause of death,' he said, and handed the glass to Dr Wright, who seized it with alacrity and stared through the lens at the area of the neck Holmes indicated. He then handed the glass to me, and I was able to see what Holmes had detected. It was a very thin reddish line around the neck, almost hidden in the folds of the wrinkled sloughing skin.

'It is the mark left by a fine cord,' said Holmes. 'Nothing else on the body could account for it. The cord itself has been taken away. It passed completely around the front of the neck. I suggest we turn the body and see what we can find at the back.' Sure enough, once the body had been turned on one side, we saw that the line extended the full circumference of the neck, with some suggestion in the markings that the cord had been crossed over at the back. Where it had bitten deep, we could see through the lens a suggestion of the twisted strands that made up the cord. 'Harry Gibson was murdered by someone who approached him from behind, and threw a cord about his neck,' said Holmes. 'He would have been unconscious in seconds, helpless, and was then tumbled into the ditch. How cruel.'

Dr Wright proceeded to open the body and confirmed that none of the signs of drowning were present. Harry Gibson had been dead when he entered the water.

'As far as we know, he was alive six days ago,' said Holmes. 'He was making his delivery rounds on the night Mr Clark was killed. He might even have died the same night.'

'It is certainly possible,' said Wright. 'It is hard to be accurate in a case such as this, even to the day, due to the temperature of the water, the changeable weather, the effect of clothing and so on. But we can see the typical changes in the skin, some bloating, and decomposition of the internal organs. I would say he has been dead about five or six days. I cannot say any more than that.'

'But Mr Sharp says the stone was placed there last night,' I said. 'He knows that because he was alerted by the dog.'

'Bodies immersed in water will tend to sink at first,' said Wright. 'A dead body, if there is air still in the lungs, may take a little longer, but it too will soon sink. They rise to the surface later, when the gases of decomposition form. Whoever placed him there might have assumed that once he had disappeared below the surface, he would not emerge until many months later in drier weather, as a skeleton in rotting rags. If the killer had returned some days later to check that the body was still submerged, he would have had something of a surprise and decided to weight it down, causing it to sink to the bottom of the ditch. The boundary stone was conveniently only a few yards away.'

'And how did the watch come to be there?'

'I can only assume that the victim stole it. Inspector Mackie is inclined to the belief that Gibson entered Spring Cottage primarily for the purpose of murdering Mr Clark, happened to see the watch and took it. Mr Overton was adamant that he knew his lad very well, and he was the last person he would have suspected of a serious crime of any kind. But people surprise us all the time.'

'Do you have anything to say regarding the fact that the body was lying face down in the ditch?' Holmes asked.

'You think that may be important?'

'Possibly.'

'I doubt it was deliberate. The murderer had come up behind his victim in order to use the garrotte, and then after the struggle, pushed or rolled him into the ditch. It was probably merely chance.'

Holmes looked thoughtful, and it was that very loud and intense thoughtfulness which showed he had other ideas.

I said nothing because I was left feeling uncomfortable. I was trying to recall something I had learned during a lecture, and I wished I had my notes with me so I could remember what it was.

CHAPTER TWENTY-EIGHT

Inspector Mackie called on us at Spring Cottage the next morning, and despite the discovery of the body and the stolen watch, he had been unable to relinquish the idea that Mrs Clark was somehow involved in her husband's death. He had long suspected that she had a secret accomplice, and finding no evidence with which he could charge me with murder, he had seized upon the theory that poor Harry Gibson was the man. To his way of thinking a youth of nineteen, with a sweetheart whom he might have intended to marry, would have been amenable to a plot to steal a valuable watch which the unhappy wife had once owned. Harry Gibson might not have been a thief by habit, but Mackie thought he might have been inveigled into carrying out a plan for a distressed lady, especially if it involved payment. Perhaps she had asked him to steal the little pearl-handled gun as well.

Mrs Clark refused to rise to the inspector's insinuations and declined to answer his questions without the presence of her solicitor. She challenged him to arrest and charge her, but of course he had nothing but suspicion. I was only relieved that he stopped short of accusing Mrs Clark of having an intrigue with the young delivery boy, which would have been outrageous. If he had hoped to wear her down and cow her into a confession, he was disappointed. Before he left, I had the temerity to ask him if he had discovered who the stranger was who had arrived at Coldwell station on the night of the murder. He admitted that he had. The visitor was the grandson of Mr Felby, the gentleman who lived at the Old Manor

House, and there were witnesses to the fact that he never stirred from the house that night.'

'You informed us earlier that Harry Gibson returned the cart to Upper Coldwell Farm after completing his deliveries, and there was a witness who saw him do so,' said Holmes.

'Yes,' replied Mackie, 'and Farmer Overton confirmed that the cart had been returned.'

'In exactly its usual place?'

'I don't follow you.'

'It would be interesting, would it not, if the cart was not replaced where it usually stood?'

'It might.'

'And it is curious that the body was found in a location which suggested he was travelling west rather than east.'

'Not especially. It suggests to me that he had an appointment at the spot where he was killed and took the cart back beforehand. He might have been in a hurry, as he still had to go to Romford afterwards.'

'What is the name of this witness?'

'I am not prepared to say.'

'I only comment that since Harry Gibson was a well-known figure with his delivery cart, it would be easy to make a mistake in the darkness if another man was pushing it.'

'Oh, and who might that have been? Not you, Mr Stamford?' Mackie saw my expression of alarm and chuckled.

Holmes decided not to question him further.

'Do you think it was Gibson with the cart?' I asked once the inspector had taken his leave.

'I take the inspector's point that it might have been. He would not have pushed it all the way to his meeting. But it is also possible that it was his killer, who replaced it after the murder to mislead searchers. It could not possibly have been you, Stamford. You are not the stuff of which cold-blooded murderers are made.'

'Thank you.'

'If it was the killer, that means he was a local man who knew Gibson's usual practice of taking the cart back to the farm, but not exactly where he put it.'

Mrs Pettigrew was especially annoyed when she learned of the inspector's suggestions. 'He never met the poor young boy and knows nothing about him. Yes, he was saving his pennies against the time he might marry, but he would never have done anything wrong to get money. Clem told me that Mr Cutter once offered him some good pay to work for him, and he did go there, but he came back before too long, saying he didn't like the way the man ran his business and he would rather do an honest day's toil, however humble it was.'

Later that day, Mr Oakes, having completed his work, called upon us and was open to the suggestion that we might all repair to the Plough for a refreshing drink. The builder was a wiry man in his forties with a shock of greying hair. We found a table in one corner of the bar room and Oakes, saying that his work had given him a great thirst, dispatched a glass of beer before we had sipped ours twice. Another was ordered for him, and, on his announcement that his labours had resulted in a powerful hunger, a large platter of bread and cheese.

'I'm surprised I wasn't called to give evidence at the inquest,' he said. 'I was doing a job in Chelmsford at the time, but the wife knew where I was, and I would have come back to tell what I knew. I can only think Clark didn't tell anyone about my seeing him. But he was making plans, that's for sure.'

'When did you see him?' asked Holmes.

'It would have been about three weeks ago.'

'Two weeks before he died?'

'I suppose it was.'

'Had you met him before?'

'No, never saw the man till then. He sent me a note telling me Sam Empson had recommended me and asked me to call the next afternoon to look at the back of the house, where there was repair work to be done. It so happened I had a job to do at the school that day, so once that was done, I went along, and he was waiting outside for me.'

'How did he seem to you?'

'Straightforward enough. I mean, he didn't strike me as behaving strangely. He was concerned about the security of the cottage, but I thought that was natural, as it was an old property and hadn't been looked after. If it had been mine, I would have been worried, too.'

'You had not done any work on it before?'

'No, never.'

'What did he ask you to do?'

'He said he wanted me to look at the mortar, by the kitchen door. There was a lock and Sam Empson had installed a bolt, but Empson told him it still wasn't properly secure because of the cracked mortar and would need extra work. He asked me to take a look and see if I could make it good.'

'Did you examine it?'

'I did.'

'And did your examination at any time involve probing the crack, perhaps with some sort of tool, or anything else?'

'No, I didn't need to. If I had been inside the house, I could have seen daylight through it.'

'Did you go inside?'

'No.'

'You didn't speak to any other occupant?'

'No, just to Clark.'

'And did you contract with him to do the work?'

'I did not. I told him straight. No amount of mortar was going to put right what was wrong with that house.'

'I have had my suspicions,' said Holmes, 'but your expert opinion would be welcome.'

'You'll have seen that dip in the soil out back. I reckon it's a cracked drain. In fact, there's a nasty smell out there which will only get a lot riper come summer. Worse than that, I think the drains, which must be quite old, are in a state of collapse. I'm talking serious subsidence that's been allowed through years of neglect to undermine the whole rear of the property. Just because we can't see under the surface doesn't mean it's a small thing. I told Clark he had better jump to it and put in some supports to shore up the back wall or the whole thing might come down. Maybe not next day or next month, but it wouldn't take long. In fact, if he wanted to have repairs done, he should start by having the rear wall demolished and rebuilt, and the garden excavated and a whole new set of drains put in.'

'That would be an expensive business,' said Holmes.

'Oh yes, and that would just be the start of it. I said to him, "Mr Clark, I won't lie, I can give you a price for the work I have described, but in a house this age, that no-one has touched in a long time, who knows what else I might find once the work starts? It could end up being twice the cost."'

'How did he respond to that?'

'Well, he wasn't happy. Then he asked me how much the house might be worth if it was sold just as it was. I had to tell him, in its present state, and with all the expenses attached, it would like as not be hardly worth much at all. Any buyer probably wouldn't trouble himself to do repairs but would tear the whole house down and build new. So he thought about that for a bit. He said the property was in his wife's name, but she couldn't sell it without his say-so. He thought he would have to break the news to her, but he said he would have to do it very gently, as she was of a nervous disposition. He asked me not to say anything to anyone about it before he had a chance to talk to his wife. He thought it might prove to be best for them to sell up and move. Then he asked me to make an offer for the property, and I said I would have to think about it and let him know. He said not to do it by letter in case his wife saw it and got upset.'

'Did you make an offer?'

'He came up to Ilford — that was last Saturday, and we talked it through and I gave him a figure, but that was just for the land, less all my expenses. He said he would think about it, and that was the last I saw of him.'

'Did Clark ask you to do any work for him at all?'

'No, none. I had told him what was what, and it was up to him to decide.'

Oakes, who had nothing further to tell us, demolished the bread and cheese, helped down with his second beer, and took his leave.

'Mrs Clark believed her husband still entertained the idea of repairing the house,' I said.

'He clearly had no intention of doing so,' said Holmes. 'He might have considered selling it, but that would have required his wife's agreement. Unless — yes, perhaps that was what he was writing at his desk. He wasn't writing letters; he was practising her signature. He must have thrown the evidence on the fire. No wonder he chose not to use the blotter. But I think it was Mr Oakes's revelation that finally decided him to leave her, taking with him whatever valuables he could lay his hands on. That meeting with Oakes was two days before he saw

Cutter and sold the effects. Cutter was supposed to call and collect everything and hand over the money, and only held back a few days when he heard that Clark was dead.'

'That was unusually respectful,' I said.

'He also knew the house would be in the hands of the police.'

'Oh, yes, of course. But what would have happened if Clark had not been killed? How would he have accounted for his sudden selling of the effects?'

'He wouldn't have needed to. Recall what Mrs Clark told us of the plans for going to Chelmsford? The birthday treat? Including the housekeeper? The ladies were to go shopping while Clark attended to business, then they were all to meet at a hotel to have tea. The little party would have set off, and then when Mrs Clark and Mrs Pettigrew were about to visit the shops, Clark would have said he was going to see to his business and would join them later for tea. Instead, he would have returned to Spring Cottage, admitted Cutter, taken his money and left. Once the ladies had done their shopping, they would have gone to the hotel for tea and waited for Mr Clark to join them. When he did not appear, they might have feared he had been taken ill or met with an accident. After making fruitless enquiries in Chelmsford, they would have returned to Coldwell and Spring Cottage, only to find an empty house.'

It was a dreadful thought.

CHAPTER TWENTY-NINE

Later that day we were having our dinner at the Plough when Sergeant Lestrade bustled in.

'Good evening!' he said. 'I was told I would find you gentlemen here.'

'Have you come to assist Inspector Mackie?' asked Holmes as the policeman joined us.

'That was not my original purpose. I came up to Romford this morning in the company of a Mr Bertram Pullan. He is the grandson of one of the ladies who was deceived by Mr Frederick Quintinfield into giving him some of her valuables. One of the items was recently found offered for sale by a jeweller in Romford, and we have been hoping to locate some of the others. Not with any success so far. I had already heard about the Coldwell murder, but no sooner had I arrived than I found that all the talk was of another killing. The result is that I have been detailed to stay on and bring the might of Scotland Yard to bear on the case.'

Holmes smiled, but not unkindly. In his eyes Lestrade was a plodder without any brilliance, but he had energy and determination.

'I have already had a conference with Inspector Mackie, who has laid all the facts before me,' the sergeant went on. 'He thinks Harry Gibson was the killer of Mr Clark, although whether that was the intended mission, or he did so when challenged by Clark, he cannot be sure. Gibson must have been admitted to the house by one of the occupants. The inspector is not at all convinced by the stories of Mrs Clark and Mrs Pettigrew, but he cannot disprove them.'

'How does he account for where the body was found?' asked Holmes. 'I assume he has examined the scene, but it must have been well trampled before he saw it. I saw no marks or deep footprints, which might have suggested that the victim was killed elsewhere and dragged or carried to the spot.'

'His theory is that Harry Gibson went to meet his partner in crime in a remote spot, away from any public thoroughfare, expecting to receive payment for his work, but the plan was never to pay him. He was killed to keep him quiet. The inspector hasn't named a suspect, but he did say that while the garrotte was a man's weapon, he wouldn't put it past two determined women to use it in concert.'

'Good heavens!' I exclaimed.

'How does he account for the watch being found in the ditch?' asked Holmes.

'He thinks Gibson had it in his pocket and it fell in the struggle.'

'No-one in Coldwell thinks Gibson was dishonest,' I said.

'He was a rare one, then. There are enough men about who will kill for pennies,' said Lestrade. 'Desperate characters who sneak up on unsuspecting victims and use the garrotte. It's quite the fashion in London. Sometimes they throw an arm around the neck from behind, but the cord is more deadly. Nasty things. I will see what I can do. For now, I will be lodging at Rose Cottage with Constable Higgs. If you have any information, you can send me a note there.'

'And if you should learn any more, we would be obliged to know,' said Holmes. He shared with Lestrade what he had learned from Mr Oakes. 'That would only strengthen the inspector's suspicions if Mrs Clark knew anything of it, but I am convinced she is telling the truth. Her husband had woven a web of believable deceit.'

Lestrade wrote in his notebook. 'I rather thought the inspector disapproved of your involvement. Far be it from me to put a senior officer right, but I did mention that your observations had proved useful to Scotland Yard in the past, and you never took any credit for it, but were content to have been of assistance.'

'I would like to meet Mr Pullan,' said Holmes. 'Would he be willing to speak to me?'

'I don't see why not,' said Lestrade. 'It's not Mackie's case, it's the Yard's, so I doubt he'd be able to object.'

An hour later Holmes and I, together with Sergeant Lestrade, were in the cosy parlour of Rose Cottage, where we met Bertram Pullan. He was about twenty-five, a neat, slim fellow in a suit of clothes which I suspected had been sensitively crafted by one of the better-known tailors. I like good clothes, and in the days of my youth I was known to gaze wistfully in the shop windows of master tailors, but never had the funds to dare enter. As I sat there in my borrowed suit, I felt terribly shabby.

'Perhaps Mr Pullan would begin by telling you something of himself,' said Lestrade.

Mr Pullan had been blotting his fingertips on a handkerchief, which he folded carefully and tucked into his pocket. 'I am the grandson of the late Edna May Pullan,' he said, 'one of the ladies who was preyed upon so cruelly by that scoundrel Frederick Quintinfield. She enjoyed a long and happy life, and I was extremely fond of her. My grandfather had made a fortune in commodities and was able to retire at the age of fifty. They were a devoted couple and exchanged many gifts of value to mark special occasions and anniversaries. One such item was a gentleman's signet ring, which my grandmother had made to her own design. It was very distinctive, and there was an affectionate message engraved inside. I have never seen another like it. After my grandfather died, my grandmother lived alone, and entertained very little company. She was eighty-five when she met Mr Quintinfield, after enquiring after some interesting pieces on display in his shop. The scoundrel wormed his way into her life; he called on her, and offered advice on the value of her jewellery. She became very attached to him and looked forward to his visits. It was not until after her death that I discovered there were items missing. Her maid told me she had seen her mistress giving them to Mr Quintinfield, but whether as gifts or simply for him to take for valuation, she did not know. I went to see him, and he insisted that they had been gifts. I was not convinced he was telling the truth and informed the police, but it was impossible to prove otherwise. My grandmother was in full possession of her faculties until her death at the age of ninety and was of course entitled to do as she pleased with her property. But due to my suspicions about Mr Quintinfield, I engaged Mr Pollaky to look into his dealings. It was he who found that there were other persons in the same position as me. Representatives of those families met with each other and eventually we sent a deputation to the police. That was when we discovered that the police had been taking a great interest in Mr Quintinfield, as there were other reasons to be suspicious of him. Soon afterwards he disappeared, and both the police and Mr Pollaky have been looking for him ever since. About three weeks ago I was visiting an aunt in Romford and chanced to see my grandfather's ring in the window of a jeweller's shop. I asked to examine it, and it was beyond doubt that it was the same one. But I have been able to discover nothing further.'

'When did the jeweller acquire it?' asked Holmes.

'About three months ago,' said Lestrade. 'But he had no record of the seller, who was a woman, and did not give her name, or where the piece had been for the last year. Quintinfield might have sold it after he had absconded or before. As it is so distinctive, we have hopes of following it back to the original sale, but it will take time and shoe leather.'

'Did you ever meet Mr Quintinfield?' Holmes asked Pullan.

'No, the only description I have is that of my grandmother, who described him as a nice young man, dark and very handsome. Her eyesight was not the best, and all men under fifty looked young to her.'

'Scotland Yard has been on the trail of this man for some time,' said Lestrade. 'Mr Pullan has agreed to come with me to look at other possible establishments where his grandmother's possessions might have been sold or are still on display.'

'I have a list,' said Mr Pullan. 'Small items such as tie pins and cufflinks, but all of fine quality. I am hoping to discover some of them, but we have not been fortunate so far.'

'It is my hope that by finding them we will not only recover Mrs Pullan's property for her family, but we will uncover some clues as to Mr Quintinfield's movements,' said Lestrade. 'We may even locate the man himself.'

'Forgive me, Sergeant,' said Holmes, 'but I have received information very recently which suggested that Mr Quintinfield has passed away. I had thought you would have been informed.'

'I have, and I can confirm that a Mr Frederick Quintinfield did die of a brain disease in an asylum two months ago. But the villain we are seeking is not he.'

'Please explain,' said Holmes.

'Mr Quintinfield was admitted to an asylum some seventeen years ago at the age of twenty. He was never released. We have examined the records of the asylum and interviewed the director, and there is no doubt about it. Whoever the man was who worked with the father and was introduced to customers as the son, was not in fact Frederick Quintinfield. The son's disease was by then too advanced for it to be possible. The theory is that the father, not liking to admit to his son's illness, might have connived at an imposture. Perhaps people were talking, and he wanted to prove them wrong. He engaged an assistant who had some resemblance to his son. That is the man we are looking for. What his real name might be, we don't know.'

Holmes nodded thoughtfully. 'I can see now why the asylum, on learning that the police were searching for a missing man called Frederick Quintinfield, were sure, despite the coincidence of an unusual name, that he could not be their patient.'

'That is so.'

'It also explains why the man posing as the son did not go to probate. He did not want to set in motion a legal process which might have exposed him. Was the estate very valuable?'

'Moderately, yes. Mainly cash and moveable goods. The shop was rented, and the father and his assistants lived above it.'

'Do you have any information to suggest where the fugitive is and what he might be doing?'

'He's a clever one,' said Lestrade. 'Probably hiding in plain sight. He can't get at his money, as he knows the police are watching his accounts. He'll be making another fortune by whatever means he can. We'll find him, I'm determined on that. They even say he killed the old father. If he had succeeded in marrying any of the ladies he proposed to — well —' he glanced at Pullan — 'we'll say no more about that.'

'How long do you intend to spend here to make your searches?' asked Holmes.

'Two days, perhaps three. I will let you know if anything is found. Are you engaged on the Clark case? Perhaps we should meet here tomorrow to compare notes. Two minds are better than one, eh?'

Holmes declined to comment.

CHAPTER THIRTY

Next morning, we took the train to Ilford for the funeral of John Clark. A cruel wind was blowing, and we secured a cab at the station to the parish church of St Mary's. It was a handsome rather than beautiful church with a long nave and square tower. A painted sign told us it had been consecrated in 1831. A substantial burial ground adjoining the eastern side was, judging by the freshness of the railings, a recent addition. The grave that had been prepared to receive the remains of John Clark was in the family burial plot, which lay in the smaller original churchyard. A path led between the graves from the High Street to the church door. As we walked along, we looked at the gravestones on either side, as people often do, reading the inscriptions and contemplating them. At the Clark family plot, we paused.

The headstone told us that Susan Clark, John's mother, had died in 1837, and her husband John senior in 1871. There were two other children, Matthew 1832–1833, and Hannah 1837–1839. The plot was well kept and there was a small wreath which had not been there long. 'I think,' said Holmes, 'that when Mr Danbury encountered Mr Clark on the train, he was coming here to lay that little tribute. There is a florist selling wreaths of that design not far from the church entrance.'

Within, as befitted a parish church, was a generous space, which made the small congregation appear even smaller. Our little party consisted of myself, Holmes, the widow, and Lily. Mrs Pettigrew had remained at Spring Cottage to prepare refreshments for anyone who wished to return there. There were other familiar faces, Inspector Mackie, and Mr Danbury.

Apart from the undertaker's coffin bearers, most of the others present were too young to have known the Clarks and were probably members of the Essex press. There were some older residents of Ilford, although whether they had come to pay their respects to the departed, or just to keep out of the cold wind, was not immediately apparent.

The coffin was in place, mounted on trestles, the widow's floral tribute and mourning card its sole adornment. As we were seated, I saw Mrs Clark's eyes gaze at the funeral wreath, as if she was beginning to regret its sentiments.

The vicar made a simple speech, the kind vicars make when they do not know the man about to be buried. He spoke of John Clark's upbringing in Ilford, his departure for London many years ago, and the recent return ending in tragedy. He trusted in the diligence and energy of the Essex police to apprehend the culprit soon and offered his sincere sympathy to the widow. Looking at the little assembly, he asked if there was anyone who wished to say a few words.

Inspector Mackie put up his hand and was beckoned forward. He squared his shoulders and looked about him. He gave an especially pointed stare at the widow, who refused to look at him. He finally fixed his attention on the little contingent of the press, and weighed his words with care, as he must have known that they would appear in the newspapers.

'I am Inspector Gordon Mackie of the Romford police. I was never acquainted with the deceased but have learned what I can of him during my enquiries into his sudden death. At present, the reasons for his murder remain a mystery, a mystery I fully intend to solve. In fact, I have every confidence that I will have the murderer in custody before long. Important pieces of evidence are coming to light every day. I would ask anyone who knows something which would assist the police in closing this enquiry but has not yet come forward, to do so. If you wish to talk to me in confidence, you may address a note to that effect to Romford Police Station at the Old Court House. Thank you.'

He sat down again, and the press men copied down his words. One of them leaned across to another and whispered, 'He doesn't know anything, does he?'

A venerable gentleman, who was sitting at the back of the church, now rose to his feet with the deliberation and care of the very aged. 'I would like to say a few words,' he said.

The vicar nodded and the man came forward, his progress assisted by a gnarled stick.

'My name is William Harris,' he said, 'and I am a linen draper. I have lived in Ilford all my life. I knew all the Clark family well, as their shop was close by mine.

'Now, there's a lot of things been said lately in this town about John Clark, and many of them are not to his credit. I won't repeat those words, because this is not the time and place to say them. And his faults, such as they were, were those of a young man, a man of ambition. But he came from good, honest, hardworking people. I knew his father, John senior, who died some years back, and he never did an unkind thing in his life, and worked every hour there was to provide well for his family. I knew his mother, too, Susan, a gentle, pious soul, who went to her maker young because she was too good for this world. There was a younger brother and sister who joined her in grace. And his uncle Elias, who went to London and so I have heard did very well in business. But John Clark never recovered from the death of his mother, and that loss meant that he grew up without the steadying womanly hand a young man should have. And that was his misfortune. He has not lived here for many a year, and how he led his life from going away to his return we may never know. But he stands before the great judge now, and we can only wish his soul may rest in peace.'

The gentleman took his place again. I glanced at Holmes, intending to make some comment on the speeches, but was silenced by the intensity of his expression, his eyes revealing the most profound contemplation, which I dared not interrupt.

There followed a funeral hymn, a ghastly dirge which few of those present engaged with, allowing the vicar to reveal the fact that he was unable to sing in tune. The coffin was then taken up and the congregation filed out to attend the interment.

Holmes lost no time in approaching the elderly gentleman who had spoken at the funeral, and I did my best to listen to the conversation without appearing to be an impertinent eavesdropper. 'If I might say so, Mr Harris, that was a very moving speech,' said Holmes. 'I did not know the deceased, I am an acquaintance of his widow, and I heartily approve your decision not to speak ill of the dead.'

'Ah well, it wouldn't do any good to anyone now, would it? I don't think the character of the man has anything to do with what happened. There's no-one but me now can remember those things, and I certainly didn't shoot him.' Mr Harris gave a brief chuckle which rather suggested he might have wanted to shoot Mr Clark but had not troubled to do so.

'You have interested me now,' said Holmes. 'I am acting for the widow as her advisor and would welcome anything you might divulge which would comfort her in her loss, and perhaps go to explain some of the things which she still finds inexplicable concerning her husband. They had not known each other very long when they married.'

Mr Harris paused and chuckled once more. 'Well, I'll tell you,' he said. 'John Clark who we are burying today was not the son of John Clark senior. He took the name when his mother married. He was born about five years before.'

'She was a widow?'

'That was what we were told, but I suspected different. She was a comely lass, but truth be told, she was not as perfect as I let on. But old John, he was very taken with her and happy to have the boy to look after as well, as part of the bargain. After she passed on, he did all he could for the son in her memory. But the boy betrayed his trust and he never got over it.'

'Where were the couple married? At this church or elsewhere?'

'Here. Not long after it was consecrated.'

'What was her name then?'

'Oh, I don't rightly remember. Something a bit out of the way. It'll be in the church books.'

Holmes said nothing but once the coffin had been lowered and all was done, he went to speak to the vicar, and they returned to the church. I was expected to attend to the ladies and so suggested a little walk about the graves to distract them. People do like to picnic in cemeteries in fine weather, but this was not the time, and all we could think of was the hot tea that awaited us at the cottage.

'What is Mr Holmes up to?' asked Lily.

'I hardly know most of the time,' I said. 'I hope he will enlighten us.'

When he emerged, however, all he said was, 'I must see Lestrade.' He said nothing on the journey back to Coldwell, but the power of his thought was almost tangible.

CHAPTER THIRTY-ONE

At Coldwell, Holmes immediately sought out Lestrade, but he and Mr Pullan were out on their mission to find lost jewellery, and he was obliged to leave a note for him on their return.

At Spring Cottage Mrs Pettigrew had set out some tea and sandwiches and cake for any mourners. Since few people had known John Clark, or if they had, deemed it not worth their while to take refreshments in his memory, it was a small gathering. Mr Danbury was there, and a young press gentleman who had been at the funeral and was rather too eager in his questioning. Holmes was silent with his thoughts and refused to be drawn into conversation.

At last, the funeral party was disbanded. Mrs Pettigrew removed the chinaware to the kitchen, and Lily and Mrs Clark stayed in their own company and did not, I believe, require the presence of men. Holmes retired to the garden with his pipe. I went to join him, hoping he would confide his thoughts. After a while, he did.

'You may think I give scant credence to the theories you advance in my investigations, Stamford, and in that you would be entirely right.' For a moment I thought Holmes was being humorous, but then I saw to my mortification that he was deadly serious. 'However,' he went on, 'I do not dismiss them altogether, neither do I forget them. Sometimes there is a faint glow of an idea, an illumination which by pure chance, enables me to see a way forward.'

'I am happy to be of assistance,' I said. 'What was it I said?'

'You once suggested that Frederick Quintinfield was one of a pair of twins, but that was not the case. Then you imagined a second family and a younger brother who was the double of the elder, but nothing came to light there. There were, however, as we now know, two men calling themselves Frederick Quintinfield, and both claiming to be the son of the pawnbroker. One of them, the genuine son, was confined to an asylum, while the other was impersonating him. Not only that but they looked very alike, sufficiently so that people who had known the son before he was confined to the asylum, were convinced that the man who took his place was the same man. Since the father did not reveal where his real son was, he was not obliged to claim a miraculous cure. The close resemblance between the two men was, I believe, because they were first cousins.'

I was amazed at this, but he went on. 'You recall Mr Danbury telling us that when he came to Essex, he was looking for a man who had arrived recently. One of these was John Clark, but he dismissed him as a suspect because John Clark was some thirteen years older than Frederick Quintinfield. But we must recall that young Quintinfield was in indifferent health and might have looked older than his years. And John Clark made an effort to look younger by dyeing his greying hair to darken it.'

'How do you know, Holmes?'

'It was apparent when I examined the body. Of course, many men dye their hair out of vanity, but that did not immediately arouse my suspicions; I merely noted it. He had not, however, dyed it for some months. Some two to three inches of hair was greying and undyed, but on the tips I detected signs of fading dye. I suspect that when he went into hiding, he cut off most of his dyed hair, but a little remained. He had no plans to re-dye his hair as there was no dye amongst his toiletries. Recall also that there were several years between the genuine

Quintinfield being admitted to the asylum and Clark arriving to take his place. The family resemblance and the father's acknowledgement of him were sufficient to convince his customers that his son had returned.'

'How did you arrive at this theory, Holmes?'

'It was simplicity itself. Mr Harris, the gentleman who spoke at the funeral, referred to John Clark's uncle, his mother's brother, as Elias. I recalled from our conversation with Mr Danbury that Quintinfield senior was also called Elias. Fortunately, the mother had married in the very church where she was later buried, and the reverend kindly permitted me to examine the registers. It showed that John Clark senior had married Susan Quintinfield.'

That afternoon Lestrade and Pullan were back in Coldwell and called on us.

'I have found your Mr Quintinfield, or at least the man who went by that name, and I can inform you that he was buried this morning at St Mary's parish church in Ilford,' said Holmes. 'He was none other than Mr John Clark who was killed in Coldwell this week.'

Lestrade was astounded. 'Mr Holmes, I beg you to explain,' he said.

'The evidence you require is in the church registers. Elias Quintinfield was the brother of John Clark's mother. He doted on his only son, Frederick, but was obliged to have him committed to an asylum.

'Some years later, John Clark came to London to work for his uncle, where he learned the business of pawnbroking. We know of his ambition, his methods of becoming wealthy by underhand means. It is possible that he did not initially intend to masquerade as Elias's son, but once the family resemblance was noted, the fiction was maintained. He took on the identity of Frederick Quintinfield. He opened bank accounts in that name. He would have used the son's birth certificate if he needed proof. He applied hair dye to appear younger. I learned from Mr Forbright, who gave evidence at the inquest, that John Clark left Ilford after stealing from his father's business. There might have been other crimes that could have been laid at his door, and a new identity would have been useful. When Elias Quintinfield died, and we have no proof of murder there, he took over the business.

'But his wrongdoings were about to catch up with him. Thanks to the determination of the families of the elderly ladies he had cheated, and the efforts of Mr Pollaky and his men, he realised that he was under suspicion. A note warned him that he was in imminent danger of arrest, and he decided to disappear. He took with him any gold and banknotes he had in hand, and items he could safely dispose of, but his other assets were held in the name he had adopted, and he dared not try and access those in case he was arrested.

'His intention was to live quietly for a time, until the trail had gone cold. He shaved his beard and allowed his hair to grow back in its natural colour. That was sufficient to change his appearance. People will return to their old haunts, and he found himself back in Essex with his original name. And then he met Miss Kenrick, a lady who had recently come into an inheritance, and whom he judged had never entertained any hopes of marriage.'

'Why did he marry?' asked Lestrade. 'He could simply have stolen from her.'

'Above all John Clark did not want to draw attention to himself. The guise of a gentleman choosing to retire to the country and live quietly suited him well. He must have looked over the cottage, and his experience undoubtedly meant he was able to identify what items were of value. He might have stolen the watch and run away, but that would have set the police on his trail again. No, the simplest and legal way to obtain ownership of the valuables was to marry Miss Kenrick.'

'It was a very quick wedding, by all accounts,' said Lestrade.

'He was known for his engaging manners. Ladies found him good company,' said Holmes. 'Miss Kenrick was alone in the world. I think she sought companionship rather than romance. There was also the security afforded by marriage to a man of property. She was not to know that there were no such properties.

'Mr Clark appeared to be perfectly settled and content. He had been telling his wife of his intention to visit Wales to see to some properties, and that he might be away for some time. He would have taken with him any items of value, including the silver watch, saying that he was having them cleaned and insured. He might well have suspected by then from his own inspection that the cottage was not a worthwhile asset, although he did not know the full situation until later. He had also discovered that the capital on the investments his wife had inherited could not be realised. Mr Clark had decided to disappear again and was laying his plans. He told his wife he would be away for some weeks, thus giving him ample time before he was missed, and any action was taken. He would have taken the train and never returned to Coldwell. Perhaps, in time, some items would have been found suggesting he had been waylaid and robbed, but his fate would have been a mystery. And Mrs Clark would have been left abandoned in a crumbling house she had insufficient means to repair, any items of real value gone.

'But then he spoke to the builder, Mr Oakes, who advised him that the rear of the house was in a dangerous state due to subsidence and urgent action was required. Had Mrs Clark learned of this, she might have demanded the property be repaired at once, something for which no funds were available, and her husband's lies would inevitably have been revealed. This hastened his plans to disappear, but he was killed before he did so.'

'How cruel!' I exclaimed.

'Men of that kind care nothing for the misery they cause. They care only about themselves,' said Holmes.

'I venture to say she is better placed as a widow than as a deserted woman,' said Lestrade.

'She is.'

Mr Pullan had been listening quietly to this. 'So our search for the villain is done,' he said. 'But the families he cheated are still desirous of finding their missing property. All of it is valuable and some of it has great sentimental meaning.' He glanced at Lestrade. 'I fear that since discovering the criminal was the main interest of Scotland Yard, there will be fewer police resources available for recovering the property.'

'You may well be correct,' said Lestrade.

'It might be to your advantage to interview Mrs Young, the landlady at the property where Mr Clark lodged when he first came to Essex,' said Holmes. 'If you take her to the local jewellers, you may find it was she who sold some of the missing items on Mr Clark's behalf.'

'I will certainly do so,' said Lestrade.

'Mr Pullan, if you would be kind enough to allow me to speak to the other representatives, I promise I will bear their plight in mind and look about me for any items I might see offered for sale,' said Holmes. 'I promise nothing, of course.'

'I can do better than that, since we have exchanged information and I carry a list with me,' said Pullan. 'I will let you have a copy.' He took a notebook from his pocket.

Holmes studied its pages and gave a little start. 'I think,' he said, 'I might know where two of these items listed might be found.'

'Oh?'

'Yes, they are in the hands of the police. I assume that their owner liked to travel?'

'Yes, she did.'

Holmes showed me the page in question. It listed a ladies' pocket pistol with a mother of pearl grip and engraved silver mounts and a pair of Persian slippers.

CHAPTER THIRTY-TWO

'What shall we tell Mrs Clark?' I asked when Lestrade and Pullan had departed.

'Everything,' said Holmes. 'It will be a long story for her to fully absorb but if I have judged the lady correctly, she is more than equal to it. If nothing else, it will serve to explain much that has been mysterious.'

I was only glad that Lily was there to support her friend.

We called a little conference in the parlour, Holmes and I, with Mrs Clark and Lily. There was tea on hand and the little brandy flask close by in case it was needed.

Holmes began by explaining that he had that very day come by some information which had enlightened him as to Mrs Clark's position. It would not be easy for her to hear, but it was essential that she do so.

'Thank you, Mr Holmes,' she said. 'I must know the truth and I am prepared for it. I have, as you can imagine, been reflecting on the discoveries that have been made since my husband's death, and I fear that he was about to desert me. In fact, if you were to tell me that that he was already married to another and my marriage to him was a sham, I would not be surprised.'

'As far as we have been able to discover, Mr John Clark was his real name and there is no trace of a prior marriage,' said Holmes. 'But yes, he had not told you all the truth about himself.'

'Please go on,' said Mrs Clark.

Holmes spoke quietly, carefully, giving the events of John Clark's life, the statements of witnesses concerning his character, his masquerade as his cousin Frederick Quintinfield, and his plan to hide from the law.

'I was part of that plan,' said Mrs Clark. 'I see it now. His kindness, his declarations of sincere affection, were all false. Even so, we might have lived here happily for longer. I suppose when the promised funds on the sale of these supposed properties did not appear, I might have become suspicious, but that would not have been for a while. He could always have claimed the law's delays, blamed it on others, assured me he was doing all he could. I would have believed him at first.'

'I think he intended to stay with you for some time, but circumstances arose which precipitated a more urgent plan to desert you,' said Holmes. He described his meeting with Mr Oakes and the builder's warnings about the state of the house. 'I believe you have nothing of value in the back bedroom now?'

Lily extended her hand to her friend and gave it a comforting squeeze. 'Nothing,' said Mrs Clark, after a long pause. 'A few items of furniture.'

'My suggestion is that you arrange to meet with Mr Oakes,' said Holmes. 'While he did not anticipate any immediate danger, it is obvious that some precautionary measures must be taken. I suggest that you remove anything from that room which you might wish to save, and keep it closed. I note that the ground floor rooms at the back consist of laundry and other offices. Mr Oakes will advise you concerning the use of those rooms.'

'Thank you,' said Mrs Clark. 'I do not have the means to carry out any repairs unless I am able to sell the watch. That is still in the hands of the police.' She helped herself to tea. 'Are there any more revelations, Mr Holmes? Do you know who murdered my husband?'

'There are some interesting circumstances I am considering, but I am not yet able to point to an individual with any certainty.'

'That horrid inspector still thinks it was poor Una!' exclaimed Lily.

I rather thought that knowing what she now knew, Mrs Clark would have been justified in dispatching her husband, but I didn't say so.

'I suppose he thinks I did it for the inheritance,' said Mrs Clark, sadly.

'I am looking forward to seeing if he changes his tune now,' said Holmes. 'After all, as he has been exposed as the man who cheated others under the name Frederick Quintinfield, and had a host of criminal connections, I ought to point out to Inspector Mackie that there might be a dozen people who would have liked to take their revenge. Little wonder that he took such pains to secure the property and chose to sleep in a room which could not be reached by climbing the ivy.'

'And what about that poor young man?' said Lily. 'Mr Gibson. Who would be so cruel?'

'I think the inspector imagined that I had hired him to dispose of my husband,' said Mrs Clark, 'and I never so much as set eyes on him.'

'He thought, although he never said it plainly, that young Mr Gibson who was, so I am told, very handsome, was carrying on an intrigue,' said Lily. 'The impudence! If anyone in this house has a secret admirer, it is not Una.'

We all smiled. 'Well, it cannot be you, Lily, as all the world would know about it,' I said. 'And as for Mrs Pettigrew —'

'Oh, but have you not seen the little herb garden she tends so carefully?'

'I — yes, of course. Ah, I understand, you refer to her devotion to her plants. That is no secret.'

'Oh, you men, you can be so dull sometimes!' Lily exclaimed. 'Do you not see what is staring you in the face?'

Spoken to Sherlock Holmes, this was quite an accusation.

'Miss Hargreaves,' he said quietly, 'might I ask you to enlighten us?'

Lily, with a shake of the head as if despairing at the stupidity of men, jumped up from the table. 'Come, I will show you!'

The weather was brighter as we emerged into the garden. 'You see the markers with the names on them,' she said. 'If you read the names, they do not describe the plants that are here. In fact, I see no sign that such plants were ever here.'

'I thought they were just decoration,' I said.

'Not a bit of it,' said Lily. 'It is a secret language. Do you not speak it?'

'I — no, I do not,' said Holmes.

'So,' said Lily archly, 'supposing, Mr Holmes, I was to make you a gift, a gift of a single red rose. What would that signify?'

'Lily, what is the name of this language?' I interrupted before my friend was subjected to any further embarrassment.

'It is the language of flowers,' said Lily. 'I have made a great study of it, as I am named for a flower. Lily means pure and beautiful. See what we have here.' She pointed to the markers. 'Fleur de luce, that is a pretty name for the iris. In the language of flowers, it signifies hope and trust, and sometimes a message. Then there is ambrosia, which is devoted love between two people. Nothing can be clearer than that. Purple bower is strength and wisdom. And finally, white jasmine is the sign of a happy marriage.'

'And the meaning is?' I asked.

'A message to the beloved: be strong and wise and we will be happily married. One can have an entire conversation consisting of nothing but herbs and flowers. But perhaps I should not have said anything. After all, it would not do to tell gentlemen all of our secrets!'

Holmes stared at the metal markers, then he said, 'I believe that Mrs Pettigrew's Christian name is Ada?'

'Yes, it is.'

'And Miss Brampton?'

'I'm afraid I don't know.'

'Iris,' I said, suddenly. Everyone turned and looked at me. 'I was looking at the garden when I first came here, and I remember Mrs Pettigrew telling me that Miss Brampton loved flowers and was named for one.'

'Mr Holmes, you must study this book,' said Lily, taking the little volume from her pocket.

To my surprise, Holmes received the book and made a little bow. 'Miss Hargreaves, I owe you an apology. I have indeed been obtuse and ignorant. The language of flowers can say a great deal, and I shall make it my study forthwith.'

To my surprise he went indoors and sat in the parlour, where he spent some time examining the little book.

'What is it, Holmes?' I asked when he finally closed the volume.

'I am very close to a conclusion,' he said. 'I believe I know the answer, but I must have one or two further pieces of information if the culprit is to be arrested and brought to justice. Fortunately, I know where to get that information. I will send a note to Sergeant Lestrade and hope to hear very soon that my suspicions are confirmed.'

CHAPTER THIRTY-THREE

After dispatching his note to Lestrade, Holmes requested an interview with the housekeeper.

'Mrs Pettigrew,' he said very seriously. His tone suggested that any attempt at concealment was useless. 'You have told us that when Mr and Miss Brampton lived here, only he and yourself had a key to the front door.'

'Yes, that is so.'

'There was a third key, but he also kept that one.'

'Yes.'

'There were only two keys to the kitchen door; Mr Brampton had one and you the other. Miss Brampton never had a key to either door.'

'She never held her own key, that is so. If she went out with Mrs Harmon, I had to let her in. They were never out late, so it was no trouble.'

'Did she ever borrow a key, if only for a short while?'

Mrs Pettigrew hesitated. 'It was not something Mr Brampton would have approved of, but he never gave any explicit orders against it.'

'Did she ever borrow a key from you?'

Mrs Pettigrew took a deep breath. 'Poor young lady, what freedom, what pleasures did she have? There were one or two times she did go out on her own. She was so afraid of her father knowing that she wore a cloak and hood to hide under. But she was hardly gone more than a quarter of an hour, to the village shop to purchase things that were needed to tend her garden. She had a few pennies of her own for needles and thread and suchlike that her father allowed her. She asked me if she might borrow the key to let herself in so I would not be disturbed in my work, and by coming to the kitchen door rather than the front door, she would not be seen with a key by any passer-by. She didn't want anyone seeing her and reporting it to him. But it was only a few minutes. And she always returned the key to me straight afterwards.'

'The key indeed,' said Holmes. 'That is what I have been looking for.'

Mrs Pettigrew suddenly burst into tears. 'Poor Miss Brampton, she had such a short, unhappy life. Her little garden was her only comfort. Then she married that awful man, who she never liked.'

'I wonder why she accepted him?' I said.

Mrs Pettigrew hesitated, dabbing her eyes on a handkerchief. 'Her father approved it. She was allowed to go out walking with Mr Rowe, so long as she was accompanied by the sister Mrs Harmon as chaperone, which was only right and proper. But I believe it was so managed by Mr Rowe that they were sometimes left alone together. She was innocent of so many things. It was Mrs Harmon who convinced her that simply being alone with her brother was enough to ensure that they were married in the eyes of the world, and that they must therefore marry before God, or she would be ruined forever.'

Lestrade had returned to London, but it was not long before he was as good as his word and Holmes received a message. 'I must go and see Inspector Mackie to advise him that he must make an arrest without delay. He is not a foolish man, and I trust he will see the sense of my argument.'

'I hope he will do so,' I said. 'Who must he arrest? Not Mrs Clark, I hope!'

'She did not murder her husband,' said Holmes.

'Then who did? And how? And why?' I asked, but Holmes was already out of the door. I had to be patient.

When Holmes returned, he looked relieved. 'If Lestrade had not had a word with Mackie on my behalf, he would have dismissed me without a hearing and then I would have had to entrap the villain myself.'

'Who?' I asked.

'The murderer was Clem Barnes.'

'But wasn't he in prison at the time?'

'That was what he wished us to believe,' said Holmes. 'He had certainly been in prison very recently. When we first encountered him, he had the typical convict pallor and his head had been shaved. He concealed the shaven head with a cap but as he walked away, I saw enough hair protruding to show that he had not been shaved in well over a week. Convicts are usually shaved once a week. Therefore, I suspected he had been released from prison rather earlier than he had led us to believe. I checked with Lestrade, and he confirmed that at the time of Mr Clark's murder Barnes had been at large for several days. What he did in those few days we do not know, but he might have been in London looking for things to steal. Then he remembered Miss Brampton, an impressionable lady whom he had once tried to court for the value of her jewels, and who had come to entertain an affection for him, one that he did not reciprocate.'

'How do you know?'

'The love messages in the garden. Flowers may have a language, but sometimes it is more obvious than that. The fleur de luce, the iris signified Miss Brampton. And purple bower, I have learned, is clematis, meaning Clem. The other flowers spoke of love and marriage.

'Clem Barnes, having just emerged from prison, did not know that Miss Brampton had married the man she always professed to dislike, and had subsequently died. He thought he might try and woo her, persuade her to take her jewels and her father's watch and run away with him. He came to Coldwell and went to Spring Cottage. How he travelled, we do not know. He might have walked or ridden on one of the farm carts. Had the little garden been allowed to fall into disuse, he might have realised that Miss Brampton was no longer living there, but Mrs Pettigrew had continued to tend it, using the markers Miss Brampton had made, in her memory. He saw it as a sign that she was still there and still entertained hopes of him.'

'But how did he get into the house?'

'I suspect that he had some proficiency as a burglar, and carried with him the items he needed: a wire, a cord, the stub of a candle. His use of material to mask his footprints he must have learned from the Cutter family. He was well acquainted with them, as we know. And the key? I think when Miss Brampton borrowed it from Mrs Pettigrew, it would have been possible for her to leave it where her suitor could pick it up and quickly take an impression so he could have it copied. How often she was able to slip out alone and have tender meetings with him, and how these appointments were made, we cannot be sure. It is possible that the miserable shed in the garden was their secret place for notes to be exchanged and the key to be left. Quite what they planned, we shall never know — an elopement, perhaps. But when Mr Rowe appeared, those romantic interludes ceased. That must have been when Barnes left Coldwell for London. When he returned, hoping to woo Miss Brampton, he thought he could just use the key to gain entrance to Spring Cottage. He didn't know that bolts had been installed, but the crack in the mortar was his doorway. He would have been able to move the bolt with the wire and open the door.'

'And fasten it again from the outside?'

'He used his cord to perform the trick described by Mr North, the locksmith.'

'And, of course, the room occupied by Mr Clark had once been Miss Brampton's.'

'Precisely. He expected to find his sweetheart there but instead there was a sleeping man. He found a silver watch and put it in his pocket. Then he looked for anything else of value and saw that there was something hidden in the slipper. He picked it up. Mr Clark must have woken. He saw the intruder and made a lunge for the gun. There was a struggle which operated the hammer and then the trigger. I am sure Mr Barnes will claim that the gun, which fired a bullet into Mr Clark's chest, discharged by accident.

'Barnes dropped the slipper, which made hardly any noise on the rug. What did he do? He didn't know if anyone else was in the house. But nothing stirred. What nerve he must have to be able to consider his position in such circumstances. He might have been tempted to steal the gun, but decided to leave it where it lay, hoping that the death would be put down to suicide. Like Mr Makeham the bonnet maker. The absence of the gun would have set the police on the path of a killer.'

'And Harry Gibson? Do you know who killed him?'

'As Barnes was leaving Spring Cottage, he might have lit the little candle stub to ensure that his tracks were covered, and check that he had left no sign he was there. Unfortunately, he chanced to meet someone who recognised him. Harry Gibson was making his delivery at an unusually early hour. They had both worked for the Cutters at one time. They might have had a conversation, and Barnes learned that Miss Brampton was deceased. He must also have been told that Gibson was early that day because he meant to see his sweetheart at Romford. Barnes knew that Gibson would identify him once the body was found. He also knew that the youth was honest and could not be bribed to keep quiet. He had to silence the witness. I believe he lured Gibson to a nearby field on some pretext or other, perhaps asking him to help rescue an animal from a ditch or some such story. And while there he crept up from behind, put the cord about his neck and strangled him, then pushed the body into a ditch.'

'Face down,' I said.

'Yes. I think he liked Gibson and was ashamed to have done what he did. He put the body in that position so he wouldn't have to look into the dead face of someone who had once been a friend. I will carry out some examination of the hessian threads when I have returned to Barts, but I am sure they will support my account.'

At this point in the narrative Holmes paused. 'And yet my case is not quite complete. Dr Wright believed that the murderer returned to the scene several days later and finding that the body had risen to the surface, put the stone on top to make it sink. When we first saw Barnes, his hands were scratched, but that was on the day before the stone was understood to have been moved.' He shook his head. 'I need to consult a text regarding the decomposition of bodies in water.'

'I remember now!' I exclaimed. 'I was at a lecture which mentioned that very subject. Dr Wright said that bodies will sink in water and only float when they decompose, but I was told of a case where a man was shot dead and fell in water face down. Unusually, the body floated at first, because his lungs were still inflated, and being face down it was harder for the air to escape.'

'By Jove, that is it,' said Holmes. 'I am indebted to you, Stamford. The stone was not moved days after the murder, it was moved to weight the body on that very same night, when it failed to sink as expected. Mr Sharp only thought it had been stolen some days later because that was when the dog, Grey, alerted him and he noticed it had gone.'

'But the dog made no fuss on the night of the murder.'

'Harry Gibson had been making deliveries in Coldwell for several years. I am sure that Grey knew him well and did not make a fuss. You saw how docile the dog was with Mrs Sharp?'

'Yes, of course.'

Holmes mused a little more. 'We know that Barnes is able to keep a cool head. After murdering Gibson, he pulled the delivery cart back to Upper Coldwell Farm, which led to the assumption that Gibson had left it there and gone on to Romford. Barnes's only mistake was he did not leave it where Gibson usually put it. He was seen by someone, but in the dim light it was assumed it was Gibson drawing the cart back.'

'Why didn't he just run away?'

'I am sure that Barnes wanted to leave Coldwell as soon as he could, but then he suddenly discovered that the stolen watch was no longer in his pocket. He had dropped it, but where? He stayed on and began working for the Cutters. He told people he had only just been released from prison, to provide himself with an alibi he thought no-one would check. He retraced his steps, looking for the watch, until he realised the one place where it must be. He had lost it during the struggle when he killed Harry Gibson. It was a risk, of course, but he went to have a look at the ditch at night to see if he could find the watch. The dog, not recognising him, made a commotion and he had to run away.'

'Sagacious creatures, dogs,' I said.

'Yes, the police should make more use of them. A well-trained dog is better than a man. An undisciplined one a greater danger. Even if Mackie dismisses my case, Lestrade will listen. As long as Barnes does not know the watch has been found, he will still be in the vicinity, biding his time to make another try at retrieving it. I expect the murder weapon is still in his pocket and it might be possible to match the marks on his victim's neck with the twist of the cord. But it is another kind of cord which undoubtedly awaits him.'

CHAPTER THIRTY-FOUR

We soon learned that Clem Barnes had been arrested for the murder of John Clark, and Inspector Mackie had earned the praise of both the police force and the public. The cord garotte was still in Barnes's possession. He had tried to throw away the key to Spring Cottage when the police appeared, but it was easily retrieved. Mrs Pettigrew was undeniably distressed, but she was well known and respected in Coldwell and there was considerable sympathy for her misfortune.

It took some weeks to unravel the complexities of Mrs Clark's fortune. When Mr Cutter next appeared at Spring Cottage, Mr Philpott was on hand to dispute his claims, but unexpectedly, the wily dealer had relented and said he would not hold the widow to her late husband's contract. I don't know why he took such a generous course of action, but I think that someone must have had a word with him and suggested that if he changed his tune, then some of his past dealings might escape close scrutiny. He weighed up the consequences and took the least risky course of action.

Mrs Clark set about having the contents of Spring Cottage properly valued, and it transpired that one of the horrid paintings in the hallway had some value once it was cleaned. Everything else in Spring Cottage was sold or given to the poor. Mrs Clark moved to some nice lodgings in Romford in company with Mrs Pettigrew. The cottage was sold to a builder and demolished for the construction of dwellings for families who worked on the land.

To everyone's surprise, the silver watch after careful examination was shown to be a forgery. The expectation of £500 became £20.

Things can sometimes turn out in a curious way, and when the affairs of the Quintinfield family were finally resolved, Mrs Clark received an unexpected letter. Mr Clark, having assumed the identity of Frederick Quintinfield, had taken control of the lucrative business on the father's death. Holmes had correctly deduced the reason why he had failed to go to probate. He had begun to salt away what funds he could with the ultimate intention of retiring on his accumulated wealth. Papers found in his London lodgings above the pawnshop suggested he was planning to disappear abroad. His plans fell apart when he realised that the police were on his trail, and he was in imminent danger of arrest. He snatched what funds and valuables he could lay his hands on and went into hiding.

The rightful heir of Elias Quintinfield was the genuine son, who at the time of his father's death, was incarcerated in an asylum. The son, knowing nothing of his good fortune, passed away in January 1877. Careful searches failed to discover any heir closer than his first cousin, John Clark. By the time he was traced, John Clark was dead. He had been unaware that he was the only and rightful heir of the property of Elias Quintinfield. Since John Clark had died intestate, all that property went to his wife. Mrs Clark discovered that she was the recipient of an unexpected fortune. Despite this, she made no show of her wealth, and resolved to live comfortably but not extravagantly. Her experience had given her a horror of being wooed only for her monetary worth.

Police searches later discovered a bank deposit box in the name of Frederick Quintinfield, and it had been operated during the time he was in the asylum, by a man who had as proof of identity a birth certificate. When the box was opened, it was found to contain jewellery and valuable silver and gold trinkets. Most of these were the property of deceased ladies who must have gifted them to the man they thought was Frederick Quintinfield. Mrs Clark took the view that these were not rightfully the property of her late husband and therefore were not hers to keep or sell. Mr Pullan assisted her in meeting the families of the ladies Clark had inveigled into giving him their valuables, and these items were returned to the heirs of the ladies in question.

Clem Barnes was found guilty at the Old Bailey of the murder of John Clark and Harry Gibson. If his only crime had been killing Clark, he might have succeeded in a claim that the gun had discharged accidentally in a struggle and received the mercy of the court. The murder of young Harry Gibson was, however, too callous for him to expect anything other than the gallows.

Mr Rowe was not a man prepared to change his ways. He cast about for another prospect and found one close to home. She was the granddaughter of Mr Felby, the retired gentleman who lived in the Old Manor House, and had come to stay with him to be a comfort in his declining years. Aged just eighteen, she had the expectation of receiving a substantial portion of his wealth on his demise. Mr Rowe, accompanied by Mrs Harmon, the widowed sister who was the very portrait of mature respectability, professed his great admiration for the young lady, and suggested that the three might walk out together to enjoy the fresh summer air. Mrs Pettigrew expressed her concern at this development to her friend Mrs Acton, housekeeper of the Old Manor House. The grandfather was warned, and on the advice of the police, provided a substitute in the form of a maidservant wearing a veil. The outcome was that Constable Higgs, who was lurking close by, after carefully judging his moment, was able to witness the schoolmaster's devious machinations. Mr Rowe and his sister were obliged to leave Coldwell in disgrace. I later heard that they ended their days in poverty, their main occupation being the writing of begging letters.

Inspector Mackie was a persistent man. He had been determined to entrap Mrs Clark and did not give up his campaign. After a short interval, judging that any grief she had experienced at the loss of her husband had faded, he began to pursue her with considerable energy. It amused her to repeatedly refuse his every approach, but after six months of tormenting him, she decided she had had sufficient revenge, and agreed to an interview. A month later, they were married. They settled in Romford, where Mrs Pettigrew kept house for them and Inspector Mackie's two children, and I believe they were very happy.

With the Coldwell killings resolved, there was only one task to complete: the disposal of the last two items of the late John Clark's estate. The little pearl-handled gun had been returned to the family of its original owner, but they were not interested in the damaged slippers. The slipper holed by a fatal bullet was donated to a police museum as a curiosity, leaving the other without a home.

'I am not sure what anyone can do with a single slipper,' said the new Mrs Mackie. 'I have been told I might keep it if I like, but I am not sure I want a reminder of my past foolishness, even if it is quite decorative. Would you like it as a souvenir, Mr Holmes?'

Holmes took the slipper and turned it over, admiring its fine, soft leather and delicate embroidery. 'I think I can find a use for it,' he said.

HISTORICAL NOTES

Coldwell is a fictional village, but the old coach road from London to Colchester still exists. My inspiration for Coldwell is Chadwell Heath, which lies between Ilford and Romford. It can be assumed that Coldwell station and London Liverpool Street station are about 12 miles apart and the rail journey would have taken about half an hour. Nowadays the train from London Liverpool Street takes 16 minutes to Ilford, 23 minutes to Chadwell Heath and 27 minutes to Romford.

Constable Thomas Simmons (born 1844) was promoted to sergeant in 1877, and inspector in 1881. In 1885 he was shot while questioning a former convict he met on the road, whom he suspected of being on his way to commit a crime.

Dr Alfred Wright (1840–1921) was called upon to attend Simmons, but he could not be saved and died four days later. Wright later performed the post-mortem examination. For further information on this notorious case, see *The Romford Outrage* by Linda Rhodes and Kathryn Abnett (Pen & Sword, 2009).

The death of George Makeham in January 1873 excited rumours of murder before it was shown to be suicide (*Essex Herald*, 28 January 1873 p. 3).

Before the Married Women's property Act 1870, married women had few legal rights. If a single woman owned real estate, i.e. land or a house, once she was married she continued to own this in her own name, but could not sell or rent it without her husband's consent. Any personal moveable property that a woman owned, such as furniture, money or jewellery, became her husband's property on marriage. Any wages a wife earned or property she inherited became the property of her husband.

The Act of 1870 provided that wages which a wife earned through her own work were regarded as her separate property. She was allowed to keep up to £200 of inheritance, and any property she inherited from next of kin. The law regarding real estate and personal property held before marriage was unchanged. The rights of wives were greatly extended by the Married Women's Property Act of 1882.

If John Clark had given a false name on the marriage certificate, he would not have been entitled to any property accruing from the marriage (Marriage Act 1836 (23)).

The Old Court House Romford was built in 1826. The gaol, consisting of four cells on the ground floor of the building, was in use by the police until a new police station was opened in 1893. The author is indebted to Havering Libraries for this information.

In the UK, registration of births, marriages and deaths, copies of which are held by the General Register Office, started on 1 July 1837. Prior to that, these events were recorded by churches in the parish records.

Charles Carne Lewis, (1832–1896) was a solicitor and coroner for South Essex.

Ignatius Pollaky, known as 'Paddington Pollaky' (1828–1918) was a renowned private detective whose office was in

Paddington Green from 1865 to 1882. He employed numerous agents. For further details of his career, see *Paddington Pollaky, Private Detective*, by Bryan Kesselman (The History Press, 2015).

Rutland was, before its 20th century amalgamation into Leicestershire, the smallest county in England.

£500 in 1877 would be equivalent to roughly £48,000 in 2023.

Holmes appreciated the ability of dogs to follow a trail (*The Sign of Four*), but he also knew the dangers, as he had once been bitten on the ankle by a bull terrier, an injury which laid him up for ten days ('The Adventure of the *Gloria Scott*').

In this book, Holmes acquires a stout jack-knife for country visits. Could this be the same one he later used to transfix unanswered correspondence to the mantelpiece of 221b Baker Street? He certainly found a good use for the Persian slipper ('The Adventure of the Musgrave Ritual').

A NOTE TO THE READER

The timeline of the events in the life of Sherlock Holmes in the canonical fifty-six stories and four novels has occupied, fascinated and sometimes frustrated Holmesian scholars for many years. The most commonly accepted year of Holmes's birth is 1854. He did not meet Dr Watson and occupy 221b Baker Street before 1881.

Almost nothing is known about his early life and very little about his education. I think it is possible that, like Conan Doyle, he spent a year at school on the continent, where he acquired his knowledge of modern languages. He is known to have spent two years at a collegiate university, which means either Oxford or Cambridge, although which one, and what courses he took have never been revealed, but he did not take a degree. The year in which he settled permanently in London is unspecified. His first recorded case is that of 'The Adventure of the *Gloria Scott*', as recounted to Dr Watson, which took place during the university vacation. Holmes had been developing his powers of observation and deduction and was known amongst fellow students for his singular method of analysing problems. At the time this was nothing more to him than an intellectual exercise. During his work on the *Gloria Scott* mystery, however, it was suggested to him that he would make a brilliant detective and that idea took hold and gave him a direction in life.

Holmes realised that he lacked the broad and varied fields of knowledge which would serve as a foundation for his mental skills. The next few years were dedicated to acquiring that knowledge, and in doing so, he created the man who burst upon the literary scene and met Dr Watson in the first Holmes novel, *A Study in Scarlet*.

In my work, I have suggested that Holmes was at university during the years 1873–75, solving the *Gloria Scott* mystery after his second year. Realising that his particular requirements could not be provided by a university course, he did not return, choosing instead to undertake his own studies. He had boxed and fenced at university and while there is no evidence that he devoted dedicated practice to either later on, it is clear that these were skills he retained. His lodgings in London's Montague Street placed him close to the British Museum where he must have spent many hours studying in the library, and he enrolled at St Bartholomew's Medical College for practical courses in chemistry and anatomy.

And that is where my series begins.

Reviews are so important to authors, and if you enjoyed this novel I would be grateful if you could spare a few minutes to post a review on **Amazon** and **Goodreads**. I love hearing from readers, and you can connect with me online, **on Facebook**, **Twitter**, and **Instagram**.

You can also stay up to date with all my news via **my website** and by signing up to **my newsletter**.

Linda Stratmann

2023

lindastratmann.com

Sapere Books is an exciting new publisher of brilliant fiction and popular history.

To find out more about our latest releases and our monthly bargain books visit our website:
saperebooks.com

Printed in Great Britain
by Amazon